CHARLIE C

and

NANCY STANLEY MYSTERY

BY

TERENCE F. MOSS

A STORY FOR CHILDREN OF ALL AGES.

1

Other works by the author.
Stage Musicals.
Angels and Kings
Soul Traders

Pilot TV Comedies.
The Inglish Civil War
Closing Time

Novels.
The Prospect of Redemption 2012
The Killing Plan 2013
The Tusitala 2015
Be Happy with my Life 2017

Stage Plays & Adaptations.
Better by Far 2018
Petroleum 2021
O.L.D. 2021

Children's books.
Charlie Christmas and the Nancy Stanley Mystery

Coming soon
The Adventures of Herbert the Turbot
The Watchmaker's Son

Terence F. Moss
butchmoss@outlook.com
Terence F. Moss on Facebook

CONTENTS

Looking back, I'm not sure whether anything that happened at Stanley Road ever really happened. Maybe the world of Enigami was just an elaborate illusion after all. Something I had created in my head to help pass the time and protect me when I was still vulnerable to the actuality of the natural world? Now, of course, I will never know. The house has gone, and all the people I met in Enigami no longer exist, if they ever did... but I was so much older then, much older then than now.

A NOTE to my younger readers about big words!!

Please ask someone older to explain any unusual words you don't like. They probably can't, but they will appreciate you asking and may give you an ice lolly.

CHAPTER 1

Charlie enters Enigami, the world of imagination.

I stretched up as high as I could on my tiptoes to lift the black iron knocker on the front door – it was almost out of reach. I thought about rattling the letterbox flap instead;

that would have been much easier and far less precarious. I also thought about peering through the letterbox into the house behind to see what secrets it might hold... but I didn't. As far as I could make out, the eye-level positioning of the hole had been deliberately chosen for no other reason than to facilitate easy peeking... *and, of course, the delivery of letters.*

I desperately wanted to lift the letter flap... but managed to resist the urge. Instead, I stretched just a little bit further and slowly lifted the heavy iron knocker in readiness...

It was at this moment that I suddenly remembered the golden rule my mother had drilled into my brain since I was six years old. She said these were words I must never forget.

"Never ever look through someone else's letterbox! It was rude and bad-mannered, and you might see something really horrible that you would never be able to forget for the rest of your life. Once you have seen something dreadful, you can't unsee it.

You must always give the occupants sufficient time to properly prepare themselves before opening their front door. It was only fair. They couldn't see what you were doing outside the door, so why should you know what they were doing on the inside. That's what doors were for. It was common decency." (whatever that meant).

She was right, of course. Mothers always are. The thought of remembering something horrible forever did worry me a bit. So she was absolutely correct in that respect. However, it still didn't stop me from wondering what was happening behind the door...

But she told me that rule when I was six years old. I am now eleven, nearly twelve, in fact, and I am not so sure any more about the horrible monsters and other things lurking behind everybody else's front door. I don't think my mother, I call her mum, by the way, was telling a fib or anything like that. She was just trying to help me understand how the world works for everybody else and how we all fit into it. I know that now, being a little older and wiser. And anyway, it wouldn't help me with my mission, which was to retrieve my football.

Of course, what my mum said, set me thinking about what other people did in the confines of their own homes. What was it that no one else should see… was I missing out on something truly extraordinary? Did they do something that my family didn't do? The older I grew, the more curious I became. I suppose that's all part of growing up, wanting to know everything about everything. Whenever I ask too many questions about things I shouldn't, mum always scrunches up her face and mumbles, *"Curiosity killed the cat."*

The flat Cat.

Then she would waggle her finger at me as if to say those were more meaningful words that I must also remember. After that, she would go back to the ironing or hide in the toilet for half an hour.

I never really understood what the words were supposed to mean. And I have only ever seen one dead cat. That was run over by a massive lorry, not curiosity. The cat was very flat; I remember that much.

I began to realise that every day my head was being filled with more things, and one day I might run out of space… I began to wonder what would happen when my brain was full.

I asked mum if the old stuff would be forgotten or would my brain get bigger - but she told me to ask dad. I asked dad, but he said he urgently needed to go to the toilet, so that was that.

CHAPTER 2

My family.

Mags's Headless Dolls

My sister, Mags, doesn't do anything unusual except pull the heads off her dollies and torment Jammin, our family cat (Jammin is mad, by the way). I once asked Mags why she pulled off the heads, and she told me it was easier to get a new dress on without a head. *"The head gets in the way"*... I thought that was a bit odd, so I decided to drop that line of questioning, just in case it led to something even more disturbing.

she would naughtely Explain

Occasionally, Jammin would jump into the air without any provocation, have a two-second screaming fit, and then fall flat on the floor before wandering off to sleep in his basket or into the garden to kill a sparrow. It was all very odd. I often wondered if that was due to dad having his nuts cut off. (Jammin's, that is.)

Jammin having a "Moment."

My mum spends her days cooking, cleaning, and watching television. She also fills the dishwasher. I asked her one day how it washed the dishes. She said there was a tiny green goblin called Dennis living inside and that he wore a raincoat and had a tiny umbrella. When Mum turned it on, Dennis cleaned all the dishes... and that was it. I believed her for years. Strangely, I never met Dennis. It seemed like an odd career choice to me, not something I would want to do. But then I couldn't fit in the dishwasher anyway. (*I did try once*).

Dennis the Dishwasher Goblin.

My father, I call him dad, goes to work every day, except Saturday and Sunday. He comes home in the evening, eats his dinner, watches some television, and usually falls asleep. That is it. On Saturday we all go shopping at Tesco's for food and other things. On Sunday, Mum and Dad stay in bed till midday and make lots of funny noises. That's all that happens behind our front door. Nothing horrible as far as I am aware.

So, I wondered, what was it that happened in other people's houses that was so different from ours? That was the question, and I was determined to find the answer. Maybe, other people had goblins coming round for lunch or a Horse chestnut tree hidden in the lounge so they could play conkers whenever they wanted. I liked playing conkers, but it was now banned. *They...* said it was dangerous unless you had a conker licence. Sometimes, in September (I remember this because my birthday is on the 23rd), I would find a few horse chestnuts in the park while out walking with mum. I would bring them home and play in the garden on my own, but it wasn't much fun. Sometimes dad would play a game - that was much better. But I wasn't allowed to tell anybody as I would be sent to prison forever.

The Mice, the Spiders and the Conkers.

One Thursday, my mum put three chestnuts on my bedroom windowsill; she said it would frighten the spiders away. We didn't get any more spiders, but the conkers attracted mice. They would play games, chasing them around the bedroom making lots of noise before nibbling the shiny brown shell and leaving lots of mess. So I don't know if that was altogether a great idea…

Now, wobbling on my toes and with some serious misgivings, I let the knocker go, but it didn't fall back. It was stuck. So, I tapped the knocker, and it fell back onto the door; it made a large bang and made me jump. I stepped back down two steps just in case.

After what seemed like a lifetime, *a very short lifetime,* the door slowly creaked open…

A huge man stood gazing down at me. He looked strangely unhappy as if he were the loneliest man in the world, but obviously he wasn't. Statistically, it was highly improbable that the world's most desolate man lived next door to me.

14

CHAPTER 3

Mortimer Stanley.

'Can I retrieve my ball, please?'

At first, I thought he was a giant, but he wasn't - I was just a lot shorter and two steps lower. He had a long grey beard that appeared to have a nest in the middle, and tiny yellow birds were fluttering around trying to get back into it. But that was only in my imagination. From time to time, I did that, when I was bored, imagine things, that is…

'Yessssssssssss?' groaned the old man glaring warily down at me with pained curiosity. He slowly strangled the word to death - stretching it about as far as was feasibly possible - almost extending it to three syllables. The tortured sound was accompanied by a small puff of grey smoke from the pipe he was tightly clenching between his teeth. I noticed his teeth were slightly brown in colour, not like mine, which were creamy white. I did wonder if teeth changed colour as you grew older. I had noticed recently that my dads were also going brown.

The grey smoke gently floated skywards, forming a tiny halo over his head before drifting away into the world of nothingness. I could sense a peculiar medieval air of concealment about him but couldn't put my finger on precisely what that was. Oddly, he continued to exhale - long after he had finished uttering the word. Then he made a curious hissing-whistling sound, accompanied by more grey smoke. It reminded me of a boiling kettle that wasn't functioning correctly.

I became concerned that the man might just keel over at any moment, stone dead from exhaustion. He didn't. But that didn't stop me from wondering, for a few brief moments, how I would explain, with any degree of credibility, the crumpled body now slumped in the doorway. The police or whoever else might arrive at the man's front door at any moment would undoubtedly ask me questions about his untimely demise, and I wouldn't have any credible answers.

So, I swiftly prepared my defence just in case. It sounded highly questionable and somewhat dubious, but it was the best I could muster in the time available. I like to be ready for all and any eventuality, something I learnt in the cubs.

"I only knocked on his door, officer. When the gentleman opened it, he said one word, hissed a bit, blew out some grey smoke, and dropped dead. I didn't do anything. Honest. I never said a word."

It didn't sound particularly convincing. In fact, it sounded ludicrously preposterous, wholly and utterly ridiculous, a complete work of fiction. If someone had described the self-same incident to me, I would not have believed it in a hundred years. Guilty of murder by surprise! Off to prison again, this time for thirty years, on top of my life sentence for playing conkers without a permit. Things were definitely not looking too bright for me.

Charlie. Banged up for life and a bit extra.

I will miss mum and dad, my sister Mags and her collection of headless dollies, Dennis the dishwasher goblin, who I had yet to meet and Jammin, my psychopathic cat. But at least I wouldn't have to worry about going to school anymore or getting a job in the foreseeable future, so it wasn't all bad.

Fortunately, the man wasn't dead, but he was still scowling at me. His expression was now one of measured disdain fused with curiosity and some presumed displeasure at having to open his front door. He also appeared to be in some pain. I wondered whether I had interrupted his dinner, or maybe he had been sitting in the toilet reading the newspaper. My Grandfather (mum's dad), Arthur Battenburg (no relation to the cake), came to stay occasionally and often sat on the toilet for hours reading the newspaper. I had heard some strange groaning noises coming from the bathroom from time to time, not unlike my parents' bedroom on Sunday morning. I did wonder if there was any connection…

I hate to be interrupted while using the lavatory, but then I never read the newspaper while I was in there, just the Beano. Occasionally, I would spend the time mulling over the incongruous thoughts that passed through my mind whenever I was suddenly subjected to unsolicited scrutiny or interrogation by a grown-up. This was one of those times.

'Who are you?' the man grunted.

'I'm Charlie,' I promptly replied. 'Charlie Christmas from next door, number three Stanley Road, Chiswick.' I tried to be as precise as I could be. He did not look like the sort of man who would tolerate tardiness or ambiguity.

'And I am Mortimer Rowland Stanley. What do you want?' he asked brusquely.

'Hello, Mister Mortimer,' I replied with the chirpiest tone I could muster, 'can I have my ball back, please?' I stared at the dishevelled manifestation standing before me that was Mortimer Rowland Stanley. He was wearing a greenish coloured shirt, dark green cord trousers - worn at the knees, lime green brogue shoes and a battered Panama hat with a Wimbledon Tennis Purple and green banner. The hat had seen better days, much better days in fact, but then so had everything else he was wearing.

Mortimer's expression morphed into what could only be described as glazed confusion. It was a slight improvement on pained curiosity.

'Bal...la!' growled Mortimer, clinically dissecting this one-syllable word into two syllables. I was beginning to see a pattern develop. His tone lifted slightly towards the end of the second syllable as if he didn't quite understand the question. This was obviously an *"idiosyncratic eccentricity"* or possibly a speech impediment; that was my best guess. My mum had explained the precise meaning of the phrase a couple of weeks earlier when describing one particular politician and his remarkable ability to talk at great length and in great detail about absolutely nothing. I had been waiting patiently for an opportunity to impress mum by integrating the phrase into casual conversation, and this was that moment, even if it was only in thought.

It reminded me of Mr Pagham-Smythe, my history teacher. He repeated any answer to a question in the manner of another question, whether right or wrong - as if casting doubt on the veracity of your reply, but he wasn't. It was unnerving, but that was just his way. For example, Mr Pagham-Smythe would ask:

'When was the Battle of Hastings?'

I would enthusiastically answer, '1066, Sir.'

He would reply, 'Are you absolutely certain about that Christmas?'

I would say, 'Yes, sir, I think so.'

He would say, 'You only think? You don't know? Are you absolutely sure there was a battle at all?'

I would say, 'Yes, sir, there was a battle, and it was at Hastings'.

He would then say, 'Correct, boy. But, you must have the courage of your conviction and the unequivocal belief in what you trust to be correct. Stand by your words. To falter… is to fail. And you will be condemned for eternity to the status of a bumbling buffoon. And we are surrounded by enough of those.'

At that point, I couldn't even be certain of my own name or the colour of my socks, and that's how it went on until I moved to my next lesson….

'My football,' I replied by way of clarification. Mortimer squinted his eyes as if in more pain – but I think maybe he was just short-sighted.

'

'I've lost my ball, can I….'

'Football,' repeated Mortimer with a strange intonation. It was as if he had never heard the word before

'Yes,' I confirmed, 'my football,' slowly leaning a few inches to my right to peer past Mortimer, down the hallway through the dining area and kitchen and into what appeared to be a dense forest in the back garden just beyond. I was trying desperately not to break the last word into three syllables by sticking an "a" in the middle and thereby giving the appearance of somebody presenting a classic example of parodic flippancy. That was something else that infuriated Mr Pagham-Smythe, students who thought they were wittier than they actually were.

'I don't have it!' replied Mortimer sharply. His reply was executed with military precision and just a tiny hint of elongation on the final word - to add emphasis - but his expression didn't change. This time his voice dropped on the first syllable. There was an odd, unexpected hint of musicality in the timbre of his voice.

'Yes, you do,' I replied with a tiny whiff of belligerency creeping into my tone. I kicked it over the wall, into your garden… by mistake … just now.

'Where do you come from?' asked Mortimer, a curious expression flashed across his face. There was no suggestion of verbal elastication this time. Not that there was much he could elasticate.

'Cheltenham,' I replied without hesitation.

'You kicked the ball all the way from Cheltenham!' exclaimed Mortimer with some surprise. His right eyebrow arched slightly, but the left one stayed perfectly still, adamantly refusing to move in tandem.

I was a tadge confused. 'No, that's where we came from… Cheltenham, we used to live there - until today - but now we don't - we live next door, and I kicked my ball over your wall, from next door… not Cheltenham.'

'It's not my wall,' exclaimed Mortimer sharply. 'That's your legal responsibility. I'm only answerable for the wall on the left-hand side, not the right. I can show you the deeds if you wish. They clearly demonstrate incontestable delineation over the ownership of and the responsibility for boundary maintenance.'

Mortimer suddenly realised he was discussing a complex conveyancing technicality with an eleven and a half-year-old boy (nearly twelve) who presumably knew nothing whatsoever about property law. He glanced around for a moment, seemingly befuddled by what he had just said, before taking a deep breath and mumbling, 'I am sorry that was inappropriate.'

His apology immediately diffused what was obviously an awkward situation of his own making.

'Right,' I replied cautiously, not really sure how the precise details of the legal ownership of the garden wall had crept into the conversation in the first place. It was a little odd, but then the whole conversation had been strained and a bit awkward. 'So, may I retrieve my ball, or could you retrieve it for me… if you prefer?' I asked.

'Retrieve,' exclaimed Mortimer, strangely surprised by my choice of verb.

'Yes, retrieve,' I replied, now in some doubt whether I had used the word correctly. Sometimes, when I was bored, I would repeat a particular word hundreds of times until it turned into a monosyllabic sound and no longer appeared to mean anything at all. Retrieve was one of those words, and I began to regret subjecting it to this ridiculously nonsensical oral torture.

'I'm sorry, but I seldom hear young people use that word; they normally say 'get.''

'Get?' I echoed quizzically.

'Yes,' replied Mortimer, 'instead of retrieve.'

'Do they?' I asked.

'Yes,' replied Mortimer cautiously.

'I see,' I replied, adopting a curious tone as if I had never heard the word before, temporarily leaving Mortimer feeling slightly disadvantaged, 'but I don't,' I added after a few moments of silence.

'So I see,' replied Mortimer.

'You can retrieve it if you want; you will know where you kicked it; I won't.'

'Thank you,' I replied. 'I'm Charles Christmas, by the way, but everybody calls me Charlie,' I held out my hand to shake Mortimer's,

'Didn't you mention that earlier,' asked Mortimer?

'I'm not sure. I may have.' To be honest, I was no longer sure of anything. My brain felt like a windmill being battered in a bad storm.

'Hmm,' mumbled Mortimer.

'My parents are....'

'Mother Christmas and Father Christmas, I guess,' interrupted Mortimer mischievously… 'like the cake?' he added that as a frivolous afterthought, obviously trying to introduce an element of glib jocularity, but it didn't quite work.

He almost smiled - but that didn't work either.

'We're not related,' I replied.

'You're not related to your parents?' queried Mortimer, sounding confused. That's strange. Are you an orphan? Did your parents adopt you?'

'No, I'm not an orphan, and I am related to my parents; they are my… parents!' I was becoming a bit puzzled and frustrated by Mortimer's peculiar assumptions. I wondered if all old people did this…maybe as they grew older, they began to lose their grip on reality. Perhaps they didn't understand innocence anymore. Maybe they began to look

23

for complicated answers to uncomplicated questions when there wasn't one to be found. *I promised myself that I would not be like that when I grew old, but then I wondered if I would remember my promise.* Dad didn't ask me silly questions, well, not many, but then maybe he wasn't old enough yet.

'I'm just not related to Father Christmas or the cake!' I exclaimed firmly, briefly wincing with confusion. I was about to say something else but then changed my mind.

'So Morti...' I asked.

'Mortimer, not Morti!' interrupted Mortimer abruptly.

'Mortimer,' I repeated meekly in a hushed tone. I was taken aback by his brusque correction.

'Yes, or Rowland if you like. My full name is Mortimer Rowland Stanley.

'Not Morti,' I asked warily?

'No, absolutely not; I hate diminutives. My parents spent a great deal of precious time choosing my names, so I see no reason to chop them in half just for the sake of expediency.

"What, chop your parents in half?" I exclaimed, but fortunately, the words never entirely left my lips.

I was not going to go back down the father Christmas relationship road again.

The words just hovered there, lingering in my mouth for a few seconds, desperately trying to escape into the world - before turning back into a wisp of air and disappearing forever.

'Stanley, is that like our road?' I asked.

'That's right. That's where the road name came from,' replied Mortimer.

'What from your name?' I asked.

'No, not mine exactly, from my Grandfather, Henry Morton Stanley. He was a famous journalist and explorer, and he used to live here many years ago, but it didn't end too well for him.'

'What happened,' I asked, now a little curious?

'I'll tell you all about it another day.'

I thought about that for a few moments.

'I will call you Mortimer, I think… if that's okay.'

'Mortimer is just fine,' replied Mortimer. 'Good, well, you had better go on through. The garden is down the hall through the dining room and the kitchen. Your ball is probably in the clearing further down or stuck in a tree somewhere.'

'Thank you,' I replied.

'Don't go too far; there's a small river down there somewhere; you'll get wet.'

'A river,' I enquired, sounding puzzled. 'We haven't got one at the bottom of our garden.'

'It's quite a long way down,' replied Mortimer, 'maybe your garden is not as long as mine.'

'Maybe,' I muttered. It didn't seem very likely, but I thought it was best to humour him. He was ancient, after all.

As I stepped out of the kitchen into the garden, Mortimer shouted, 'take no notice of Daisy.'

'He's very shy and a bit nervous around strangers, but he's completely harmless.'

'Who's Daisy,' I casually enquired?

'My cat,' replied Mortimer, 'he's quite big; you can't miss him.'

'Okay,' I replied, but my voice faded into the distance as I disappeared into the undergrowth. I did wonder why Mortimer referred to his cat called Daisy as he… maybe he was just a bit muddled.

CHAPTER 4

Daisy.

The garden was overgrown with many strange plants with enormous leaves - and there were flowers I had never seen before. Numerous incredibly tall trees towered way above me, almost touching the sky.

It felt more like the Amazonian rain forest than a residential garden in the leafy suburbs of upper Chiswick. At this point, I should mention that I have never been to the Amazon rainforest, but I have seen it on television. For some reason, the tropical nature of the garden didn't surprise me. I was half expecting something unexpected, and this was ……

A narrow winding pathway had been mown through the grass, which eventually led to a large clearing that had also been cut. In the middle, a garden chair, a large multi-coloured parasol, and a small rattan table. The uncut area of grass around the edge stood about eighteen inches high. I couldn't see my football, so I began searching in the overgrown area.

Something had flattened a large area of the grass about six feet from where I was standing, so I made my way towards it expecting to find the ball, not what I saw when I entered the clearing. The ball wasn't there, but Daisy was - asleep. I had never seen one in real life before, not outside of a zoo, but I was pretty sure this wasn't a cat, not by any stretch of my imagination, not even a large cat… it was a fully-grown African lion.

Charlie stumbles on Daisy, "the cat?"

I mumbled a few choice words under my breath that my mother would not have approved of, but they were the only words available to me at that moment.

I decided to backtrack as quickly and quietly as possible and return to the clearing where the chairs and the table were. From there, I could run back to the house, but Daisy suddenly opened one eye and, on seeing me, obviously had other ideas. She opened the other eye and immediately sprang to her feet, not taking either eye off me for one second.

My legs had decided to stop working. I stood looking at Daisy, utterly petrified and wondering how long I had left to live. What I didn't realise was Daisy was also frozen with fear, unable to move in any direction. It was a stalemate with neither of us fully appreciating the other's situation, neither realising the other was more terrified. We stood motionless for what seemed like a lifetime but was, in fact, only about ten seconds before Mortimer arrived, calling out Daisy's name. Daisy tentatively edged his way sideways around the area of cut grass, looking like a dressage horse performing a side-pass at a gymkhana. I thought she did it rather well. I almost smiled at her skilfully elegant performance, but my face stubbornly refused to respond. It was stuck.

Charlie and Daisy are wondering...

Daisy eventually arrived alongside Mortimer, but not for one moment did she take her eyes off me. She sat down on her rump with her two front paws supporting her body, watching me intensely with one eye and Mortimer with the other.

Daisy was still petrified, but I didn't know this. I still thought she was deciding on the best way to eat me. This concerned me… quite a bit.

'He's perfectly harmless,' said Mortimer.

'Is he?' I replied, not for one moment believing Morti.

'Yes. And he has hardly any teeth left, just in case you were wondering.'

'He!' the contradiction suddenly occurred to me again….. 'You keep calling him Daisy,' I blurted out.

I have no idea why I brought up the matter of Daisy's ambiguous gender at that particular moment. Sometimes, logical thinking completely passes me by.

Daisy's gender obviously wasn't going to make any difference as to whether he would eat me or not. My brain doesn't work properly in this type of situation. Mind you, I haven't found myself in this type of situation very often; in fact, not at all.

'I prefer Daisy,' replied Mortimer.

'That's a girl's name,' I replied.

'He doesn't know that,' said Mortimer with a casual shrug.

'He might now,' I cautiously suggested.

'No, he won't. He doesn't understand much English or any language come to that, except maybe a bit of Swahili - his parents originally
  came from Africa.'

'Oh?' I said, wondering why coming from Africa would make any difference to a lion's ability to understand any language. As far as I was aware, all lions came from Africa, and none spoke English.

I was still feeling uneasy about Daisy and suddenly overwhelmed by an unexpected desire to go to the toilet, but that wasn't going to happen anytime soon. My brain was conjuring up visions of me running away and Daisy pouncing on top of me.

'Daisy, say hello to Charlie; he could be your new friend,' suggested Morti, 'He's looking for his football.' Mortimer articulated this as if he were talking to an idiotic three-year-old child.

'Daisy smiled warily, waved his paw at me, then purred gently.' I still desperately needed the toilet.

For a moment, I wondered if I had fallen asleep and this was all some strange Alice in Wonderland excursion.

I reasoned that it had been a hectic few days with moving house and everything, and maybe my brain was just worn out, which could account for the hallucination.

Where did that come from? Wondered Charlie.?

But it wasn't a daydream or a nightmare; this was actually happening.

'Daisy, go and find Charlie's ball,' said Mortimer while patting Daisy on his head.

In the blink of an eye, Daisy bounded off into the undergrowth, found the ball and knocked it into the air. It landed on my head.

'So he does understand English?' I muttered, suddenly becoming aware of the ridiculous nature of the conversation.

'A bit.'

'Oh,' I replied, 'I see.' But I didn't, not really. It didn't make any sense at all.

'How do you keep a lion in your garden?'

'The same as any other pet,' replied Morti, as if Daisy were a harmless tortoise, which he definitely wasn't.

'But she could escape,' I replied. I was still trying to make sense of a very curious situation that was becoming curiouser as the minutes passed.

'He. Daisy's a he,' corrected Mortimer.

'Sorry, my apologies,' I replied, glancing at Daisy, 'it's all very confusing.'

With a tiny nod of his head, a smile, and an upturned paw spread open, Daisy acknowledged my apology, making a high five gesture. I found that inexplicably unsettling.

I was also puzzled by Daisy's apparent understanding of what was being said. I looked at Mortimer in astonishment expecting an explanation, but none was forthcoming.

'He could, but why would he?'

'Why would he what,' I asked?

Daisy's a he, not a she!

'Escape, you said he might escape,' replied Mortimer.

'Because that's what all animals do, try to escape… Don't they?'

I added the question as an afterthought without really thinking about it.

'Do they?' asked Mortimer, looking at me with an expression that clearly questioned my assumption.

'I thought so,' but I was now a little unsure whether all animals did try to escape from captivity. We have a cat and a dog at home, and they never tried to run away. I began to wonder what captivity actually meant.

'But why try to escape?' asked Morti, 'he has everything he needs here. It's a big garden with decent walls down to the edge of the water, so he is safe, and it has everything he wants, and he can go for a swim whenever he likes.'

'Surely, he should be in a zoo or back in Africa; that's the proper place for him,' I asked

'He wouldn't like Africa, too many wild animals, and I don't think he would like the heat that much. He likes to keep himself to himself most of the time, and he has a few friends here; he seems very happy with them.'

'Doesn't like wild animals or the heat - are you sure he's a lion?'

'Oh yes, he's definitely a lion,' mumbled Mortimer.

'And should he be swimming in the Thames?' I asked.

'It's a little stream, not the Thames, just a small meandering backwater.'

'Where does it go?' I asked curiously.

'Where does what go?' asked Mortimer cagily.

'The stream.'

'Into the...' Mortimer hesitated for a moment, 'the River Thames, eventually.'

'So he is actually swimming in the Thames.'

'If you put it like that, yes, I suppose he is.'

'How else should I put it?' I asked, 'I think I'm being bamboozled.'

'Bamboozled?' exclaimed Mortimer with a hint of naughtiness spreading all over his face.

'Yes, hoodwinked, deceived,' I replied sternly.

'Hmm, not really. I just forgot that's all,' replied Mortimer with a hint of naïve innocence.

'Until I asked.'

'Yes, I suppose so.' Mortimer was dithering a bit, obviously trying to avoid the issue.

'He could eat somebody while out swimming?' I suggested, 'that would be horrendous.'

'He doesn't like meat,' replied Mortimer with firm assurance.

'A lion that doesn't eat meat,' I replied incredulously, 'that's all they feed them in the zoo. I've never seen one eating strawberry yoghurt.'

'Actually, Daisy's a vegan,' replied Morti, 'and this isn't a zoo; it's my garden.'

'A what?' I asked, not sure if I had heard that correctly.

'A vegan,' repeated Mortimer. He only eats vegetables and the occasional cheese omelette… on special occasions.'

'Vegans don't eat dairy products.'

'He doesn't know that, and it's only the odd omelette.'

'Special occasions?' I queried with some trepidation.

Daisy had an unpleasant aroma issue.

'Fridays.'

'Fridays? Why Fridays?' I asked.

'I have battered sprouts and chips, but they make Daisy fart, so he has an omelette.'

I didn't reply. There was no point. And anyway, I was still trying to get my head around Daisy being a Vegan.

'And he wouldn't like the zoo,' continued Mortimer, 'he's very shy and likes his privacy. All those people glaring at him every day would drive him bonkers.'

'You'll be telling me next that you've had a cosy little chat with him about the zoo option,' I suggested this somewhat whimsically.

'Not exactly, but we do understand each other.'

'Do you?' I asked. I wasn't so sure about that.

'Yes.'

'How long has he been here?' I asked, still trying to get my head around this strange situation.

'How long has he...' Mortimer's voice trailed off as he gazed upwards for a moment, obviously deep in thought.

Daisy, who was now lying down on the patch of cut grass, attentively listening to the conversation, tapped his paw twice on the grass; after a few seconds, he tapped another six times. I could feel the gentle vibration through the ground.

'Twenty-six years, yes, that's about right,' muttered Mortimer, without the slightest suggestion of wonderment at Daisy's arithmetical gesture, 'That's what I made it.'

My mouth fell open, and my eyes squinted in astonishment as I reran the moment in my head before cautiously questioning... 'twenty-six years?'

'Yes,' confirmed Mortimer with a quick smile.

Daisy nodded and smiled as well; this was even more disturbing.

'Can Daisy count?' I enquired gingerly, hardly believing I was

actually asking the question.

'He's not bad at mental arithmetic.'

'Not bad!… isn't that strange?'

'He can't do any algebra, or quantum mechanics, now that would be clever, and anyway, nearly everybody knows how old they are.'

I didn't know how to respond to that, so I didn't.

Mortimer gazed up into the trees in wistfully reflective meditation.

'Before Daisy, there was Muriel, Daisy's dad. She was a he as well. As far as I can remember, there have been lions living here since 1890, when my Grandfather brought four home from Africa. Obviously, that was before my time, but I have some photographs that were taken in the garden, a few with his wife, Dorothy. He gave her the lions as a wedding present.'

'That was different,' I mumbled.

'Yes, I suppose it was,' muttered Mortimer, sucking on his pipe and blowing more smoke out through his teeth.

'My dad gave my mum a canteen of cutlery when they were married. Mum always mentions that at Christmas when she gets it out. Then she smiles at dad to remind him about the gift.'

Mortimer pondered over that for a moment. 'That's nice.'

'Not as nice as having your own lions,' I replied. 'I always thought the cutlery set was a bit boring, and now I know it was incredibly boring… uninspired, you might say.'

'Uninspired, is that what your mother said?' queried Mortimer

'No, she would never say anything like that.

But occasionally, I might just catch a glimpse of her in an unguarded moment as she was laying out the cutlery, and I would see something else, something deep down in her eyes, and I would wonder what she was thinking. I never asked… perhaps she would have preferred lions….'

'That's remarkably perceptive and curiously insightful,' said Mortimer, intrigued by my observation. He half-smiled as he spoke.

'Insightful?' I queried.

'Yes,' replied Mortimer, ' as in…'

'I know what it means,' I rudely interrupted, 'I was just surprised you came to that conclusion.'

'I was only listening to your words,' replied Mortimer.

'Do you always listen to the words?' I asked.

'Not just the words, but what's between them and behind them, that's where the truth often hides.'

'I haven't told you any lies,' I snapped reassuringly.

'I didn't say you had, but maybe there is more to it. That's all. Maybe you are seeing something else.'

I thought for a moment… 'Maybe, I'm not sure.'

'Can I bring my sister Mags round to see Daisy?' I asked after a brief pause in the conversation.

'I'm not sure if that's a good idea. Your parents might not be too happy if she tells them you come round here to play football with a lion.'

'I will ask Mags to keep the secret.'

'You shouldn't keep secrets from your parents.'

'No, maybe not,' I conceded after a few moments of careful deliberation. But I will tell them about Daisy when they're ready to hear it, but maybe I won't bring Mags around, not just yet.'

'Um,' said Mortimer, quietly agreeing with my suggestion. 'Would you like a cup of tea?'

'Yes, please,' I replied, smiling.

'Right. I will go and make it. Will you be alright with Daisy?'

'Will he eat me?' I asked, but not with any real conviction. I was feeling more comfortable with the situation and no longer felt the desperate urge to go to the toilet, so that was good.

'He might lick you to death, but he won't eat you, and he's still a vegan.'

'Vegetarian, actually,' I corrected.

Mortimer smiled at my picky critique, 'vegetarian?' he queried?

'Technically, vegans don't eat eggs… unless..'

'Fair enough,' interrupted Mortimer, 'I don't think they eat skinny little boys either… fortunately.'

Listening attentively to our conversation, Daisy immediately flashed me a gummy expression of resigned acceptance. It was oddly reassuring. He had two teeth at the top and two at the bottom, but they didn't engage properly. There was no way he could eat me even if he wanted to, and I think he knew that. In a way, I found this comforting.

'Okay, I think I will be alright,' I replied. 'But if Daisy does eat me, you will have to explain where I've gone to my parents.'

'No problem,' said Mortimer smiling. Would you like some chocolate biscuits with your tea?'

'Yes please,' I replied.

'Daisy likes a choccy biscuit with his tea,' added Mortimer.

'Does he,' I replied somewhat indifferently; nothing much surprised me anymore.

Mortimer returned to the house, and I sat down in the deckchair.

'I don't like algebra,'... muttered Daisy.

When Mortimer was out of earshot, Daisy sat up, turned to me and whispered, 'I can do algebra.' He giggled for a moment.

'What!' I exclaimed. So shocked by the declaration that I nearly fell over backwards. 'You can speak!'

'Yes,' affirmed Daisy in a casual, matter-of-fact manner as if it were perfectly normal. He scratched around in his ear for a few seconds and picked something out, which he gazed at in puzzlement for a moment before flicking it into the air. He watched whatever it was fall to earth.

'But Morti said you only had a scant understanding of English.'

Daisy finds something odd in his ear.

'Yes, he would. I was a little put out by him saying I couldn't do algebra, though. I can do it - I just don't like it. It doesn't seem to have any purpose, so I pretend I don't understand... oh, and the reason I wouldn't eat you is not just because I'm vegetarian, it's because I've lost most of my teeth.'

'So... you would eat me if you were starving?' I asked with some trepidation.

Daisy's teeth had decided to go on a long holiday.

'Maybe, if I had more teeth,' he grinned at me, 'but it would be a real problem.' He pointed at his four misaligned teeth. 'I had a sweet tooth…. once… then it fell out, closely followed by all of his mates, except for these four rebels who refused to leave, fortunately. Otherwise, I'd be sucking my food through a straw… ahhhhhhh'

'Oh,' I replied, not sure whether or not I should be concerned.

Daisy looked at me for a moment as if sizing up the tasty bits…

'No, not really. Only joking,' interjected Daisy, with a naughty smile, 'do I really look like a cannibal?'

I slowly waggled my head in a circle; it was neither a nod nor a shake.

'I suppose not, but then I've never met a lion that could talk before.' I was still a little wary. 'Does Morti know you can talk?'

'No, because he won't be able to hear me; only young people like you can hear me. He's too old.'

'Why is that?' I asked. I was intrigued by the curious declaration.

'I'll explain it to you one day, soon,' replied Daisy in an odd cryptic tone.

'But lions can't speak.' I was still stunned by the revelation.

'You said that already,' replied Daisy

'But you can't...' I was being very insistent, but Daisy just kept nodding his head in defiance.

'We will just have to agree to differ on that for now, okay?' suggested Daisy.

'I still think this is all a bad dream. I must have eaten some cheese last night that had gone mouldy.'

'Well, I'm sorry to shatter the allusion, but...' Daisy smirked at me. His large brown eyes grew even larger, with a hint of smugness as he smiled, 'it's not a dream... this is real.'

'Oh,' I replied. I took a deep breath and waited a few seconds before continuing the conversation.

'So, how did you learn to talk? Who taught you?'

'My dad, Muriel mainly, and some I picked up from the telly.'

'The telly?' I was still having a problem taking this in.

'Well, there wasn't anybody else; I couldn't ask him,' Daisy nodded nonchalantly back towards the house, 'If he could hear me, I would never hear the end of it. He'd be nagging me every day over my grammar or syntax, and before I knew it, he'd be giving me spelling tests. Bugger that.'

'I can understand all that, but why choose me to talk to?'

'Are well you're different,' said Daisy

'How?' I asked.

'You're just a bairn,' said Daisy.

'A bairn… what's that?'

'A bairn's a child. Something I picked up from Taggart.'

'Taggart, what's Taggart?'

'It was a Scottish detective series on the telly a few years ago.'

'Was it?'

'Och, Aye.'

'What?'

'Och Aye, it means yes in Scottish,' said Daisy.

'Does it?' I wasn't convinced and was becoming even more baffled by the conversation. In particular, I couldn't understand why the Scottish should have two words for one of ours… I wondered if it took much longer to talk to someone from Scotland…

I suddenly saw a vision of Daisy in a kilt doing a highland fling and playing the bagpipes…. It was very frightening.

'Oh yes,' replied Daisy with a Scottish accent.

'I'm not a child anyway,' I replied indignantly, 'I'm nearly twelve.'

'Are you really,' asked Daisy?

'Yes… but I still don't understand why you are speaking to me but not Morti.'

My frightening vision

I wouldn't call him Morti if I were you... he'd be... Daisy flashed an enormous grin as he answered... 'he'd be... mortified!' Daisy immediately collapsed on the grass, on his back, laughing at his silly pun and waving his paws in the air.

I looked on, pan faced and mystified as to why Daisy was rolling around laughing.

'Is that funny?' I asked, 'I don't understand.'

'I'll explain it later; it might take a little time.'

I flashed Daisy a curious expression. 'So why are you talking to me?' I repeated.

Daisy thought that was very funny.

'That's simple… no one would believe you if you said you'd met a lion, let alone one that talks. They'd think you'd gone soft in the head.'

'Hmm,' I mumbled, quietly mulling over Daisy's unflattering comment.

'Charlie,' continued Daisy in a tutorial tone, 'I know I'm a man-lion

by the way, not the other sort, just in case you were wondering.' He adopted a manly pose for a few seconds, but it wasn't particularly convincing.

'It did cross my mind,' I replied, 'but why haven't you mentioned it to Morti?'

'I've just never bothered, well I couldn't, could I. I have to humour the old codger from time to time; his brain is a bit fuddled these days.' I was beginning to see a pattern develop. According to Daisy, everybody seemed to be going a bit loopy except Daisy.

'You call him Morti?'

'I don't actually talk to him, so no. But I wouldn't suggest you do. He doesn't like the nickname.'

'Yes, he did mention that,' I replied.

'But I can talk to you. If you told your parents or anybody that we'd had this little chat, they would take you straight to the funny farm to have your bumps read.'

'The funny farm?' I queried.

'Where they keep all the idiots and dum-dums.'

'Oh, I see. I don't think you can say that anymore.'

'No?' asked Daisy, sounding intrigued, 'why not?'

'It's not politically correct. People can't say the truth anymore. It's against the law. But you can say anything you like, as long as nobody understands what you are saying.'

'That makes a lot of sense, not,' replied Daisy sounding confused. 'I'm not people anyway; I'm a lion.'

'One that talks,' I swiftly added.

'Maybe, but only to you; I'll go all dumb and stupid if anybody else turns up expecting to have a chat.'

'I don't think you can say that either.'

'What, that lions are dumb and stupid?'

'Yes.'

'But we are, well, most of us are, not me obviously.'

'I could tell Mortimer you been keeping this a secret from him,' I suggested.

'But why?' asked Daisy, 'I trust you.'

'Because….,' but I couldn't think of a good reason.

'Look, you can come round here whenever you like, and I can show you my world, but only if you keep my secret.'

'Okay,' I replied.

'Just tell Mortimer you are going to play football with me. He's getting too old to chase a ball, so he'll be happy if you come round anytime.'

'Tomorrow then,' I suggested.

'Great, I'll see you then. I can take you out in Morti's rowing boat if the weather is nice.'

'Morti's got a boat?' I asked, looking surprised yet again, but I can't row.'

'No problem, I can,' replied Daisy.

I went quiet for a moment. I couldn't decide whether going out in a boat with a talking lion who would be doing the rowing was of more concern than the fact that I was having a meaningful discussion about the proposed venture with the lion.

I would definitely need to check the cheese wasn't mouldy once I got back home.

'So, who's for tea and bickies,' asked Mortimer, who had just returned. He had another deck chair tucked under his arm.

'Yes please,' I replied.

'I've brought another chair. If you could grab it?'

I took the chair from under Mortimer's arm and set it up.

Mortimer sat down, poured out two cups, and put some in a large saucer. He placed the saucer on the grass and then offered me a chocolate biscuit.

'Take two; one is never enough.'

'Thank you,' I replied. I took two.

'Tea, Daisy,' said Mortimer patronisingly, 'there's a good boy.' Daisy wandered over and smiled at Mortimer, then smirked at me as if to say, '*See what I mean about the old codger going soft in the head?*' I got the message.

Daisy slurped the tea in the saucer, then glanced up at Mortimer, expecting his chocolate biscuit, but it never came. Daisy was a bit put out by that and glanced at me to see if I might give him one of my biscuits, but I popped the last one into my mouth and just smiled back as if to say, *'These are my biscuits, you will have to ask Morti if you want one.'* Daisy shrugged with disappointment and continued slurping.

'So you got on alright with Daisy then?' asked Mortimer while patting

Daisy on the head.

Daisy winced with embarrassment.

'Yes, we got on fine,' I replied.

'He didn't try to eat you then?' There was a mischievous glint in Mortimer's eye.

'Soon,' muttered Daisy licking his lips and opening his eyes wide. I smirked. I knew Daisy didn't mean it.

'No, I must have been lucky; he obviously wasn't that hungry today, or maybe I was the wrong flavour?'

I was beginning to understand Mortimer's sense of humour, so I thought I would play along.

'Maybe you should give him a banana as a treat, especially as he didn't eat me,' I suggested. I glanced at Daisy playfully. Daisy had finished slurping his tea and sat back down on the grass.

Daisy glanced at me as if to say, *'I'd rather have a double cheeseburger than a banana if it's all the same.'*

'I'll go and get him a banana,' said Mortimer, 'Daisy loves bananas.' Mortimer wandered off back to the house.

'I hate bloody bananas,' mumbled Daisy after Mortimer was gone. 'I was looking forward to my choccy biscuit.'

'You shouldn't swear in front of me; I'm just a child,' I replied reproachfully. 'Bad language can do irreparable harm to an impressionable mind.'

'Can it?' queried Daisy, sounding surprised.

'Yes. I could turn out to be a mad scientist who wants to destroy the

world… and all because you swore in front of me, had you thought of that?' Daisy flashed me a concerned expression.

'I hate bloody bananas,' mumbled Daisy

'Destroy the world?' repeated Daisy with a curious expression that sort of said, "*I wonder where this is going; surely that's a bit over the top for one bloody swear word.*"

'And barbeque all the lions in it,' I added this just to add a personal dimension to the warning and give it a tiny edge. Daisy took no notice.

'But I do hate them,' snapped Daisy after a few moments. 'Morti can stick the banana up his bum for all I care.'

'Daisy!' I exclaimed. Bum wasn't exactly a swear word, but it had the same effect in this instance, 'You're a vegetarian, you love bananas.' I chanted this in an annoyingly childish sing-along tone. I was becoming more confident and beginning to feel more at ease with the situation, as well as developing a stronger sense of self-assurance.

'No, I don't,' said Daisy. 'That's all Morti ever gives me, bloody vegetables and fruit. I should have eaten you when I had the chance.'

I waggled my finger reproachfully at Daisy. 'Now I can see your true colours.'

'Nah, maybe not,' replied Daisy smirking. 'You're all skin and bones. I need meat!' Daisy smiled with a naughty grin.'

'Oh,' I said, now looking a little concerned.

Daisy started laughing. 'Had you going there, didn't I?'

'Had me going?' I queried, pretending not to understand.

'Had you worried there for a minute?' continued Daisy.

'No,' I replied assertively.

'Yes, I did. You thought I was sizing you up for lunch.'

'Well…' I muttered quietly, now not quite so self-assured.

'I was only having a laugh, getting my own back for not getting a choccy biscuit. I was really looking forward to that.'

'It's not very funny,' I replied, gently scolding Daisy. 'It's not my fault you didn't get a biscuit; it's your fault for not speaking up when you had the chance.'

Daisy dropped his head for a moment, 'I won't do it again, I promise,'

'Apology accepted. Now, what about that boat trip you mentioned?'

'Tomorrow, we can do that tomorrow,' replied Daisy.

'Good, I'm looking forward to that. I had better be going home now. We'll be going to Tesco's for some food soon… and I will have to remind dad to get some… bananas.'

Charlie says goodbye to Daisy.

Daisy smiled and kicked over the football. 'Don't forget your ball.'

'See you tomorrow,' said Daisy.

'Yea, tomorrow,' I confirmed.'

I smiled and then walked back to the house, waving goodbye as I left. Daisy waved back.

I said goodbye to Mortimer and walked back home. It had been an interesting day. Definitely one I wouldn't forget in a hurry. The days ahead were going to be different from what I had been expecting, and I wondered just how unusual they would be.

CHAPTER 5

Playing football with Daisy…

'Can I go next door to play with Daisy? She likes to play football.' I thought it best not to mention that Daisy was a lion. It seemed less problematical.

'Yes, after breakfast,' replied mum, 'are you sure Mr Stanley won't mind?'

'No, I did ask him yesterday, and he said it would be fine.' I hadn't, but I didn't think Morti would object.

'Okay. But be back by three o'clock for dinner, and please don't be late.'

'No mum,' I replied, quickly gobbling down the last piece of toast.

'Do you think Charlie going next door again is alright,' asked mum, glancing at dad?

'We've still got a lot of unpacking to do,' said dad, 'so it's probably best if he is out of the way for a few hours. I spoke to our neighbour last night; his name is Mortimer Stanley, by the way. He seems nice enough, and he doesn't mind Charlie going round. From what I could make out, he lives with his daughter, Daisy. Charlie appears to get on quite well with her; apparently, she likes football.'

'That does seem a little odd; I thought he would prefer playing with other boys,' said mum.

'He probably will once he gets to know some at school,' replied dad.

'Yes, I suppose you're right,' said mum. She continued eating her toast.

I always thought it was a little strange when they spoke about me as if I wasn't there. I looked at each of them as they spoke and smiled, but it didn't seem to make any difference. Sometimes, I wondered if maybe I had become invisible, even imagined I wasn't really there at all, and that life was all one enormous illusion....

They were mistaken about Daisy; somehow, dad had gotten the wrong end of the stick, and mum had just gone along with it.

'Daisy's a cat, actually.' I lobbed this into the conversation to attract some attention.

'A cat?' replied dad, slightly startled, 'Are you sure?'

'Yes, I think so. I do play with her when I go round.'

All of a sudden, I was no longer invisible...

I didn't feel overly inclined to correct their misunderstanding about Daisy but mentioning in advance that she was a *"cat"* would hopefully soften the blow for the day they eventually found out she was, in fact, a fully grown lion. That day would inevitably come. They always do, in my experience. I was probably pushing my luck, but as long as Daisy didn't eat me, which was becoming more and more unlikely, there wouldn't be too much of a problem... But of course, there was one other thing I had forgotten to mention.

I finished my toast and tea, put the dishes into Dennis's little house and left mum and dad chatting about Daisy, the cat that played football.

I knocked on Mortimer's door, and Mortimer opened it. 'Hello Charlie, have you come to play with Daisy again?'

'If you don't mind Mortimer,' I replied.

'Not at all. It gives him a bit of exercise, running around with you. I'm getting too old to chase him these days, and I definitely can't climb the trees anymore.'

'Does he climb trees,' I asked. For some reason, I hadn't thought of Daisy as the tree climbing sort of lion, but of course, that was absurd. All lions climb trees. But then, most lions didn't do arithmetic, so he wasn't exactly like most other lions.

'Oh yes, and he swims a bit. He likes to keep active.' Mortimer nodded at me to go on through to the garden.

'I'll bring a cup of tea or some squash through later if you like and a banana for Daisy; he likes bananas.'

I grinned about the banana but didn't say anything. I thought that was best.

'Thank you Mortimer,' I replied as I wandered off down the pathway.

'Daisy!' I shouted as I arrived at the patch of mown grass.

'I am waiting for a low flying passing Cheeseburger.'

Daisy didn't reply, so I went deeper into the garden. I shouted again. 'Daisy! Daisy, where are you?'

'I'm up here; no need to shout.'

I looked up. I could see Daisy was halfway up an oak tree, casually laying back on a branch with his front paws behind his head, wearing sunglasses and gazing into the sky.

'What are you doing up there?' I asked.

'Catching a few rays, Chas,' replied Daisy.

'Catching a few…'

'Sunbathing,' clarified Daisy.

'Sunbathing?' I was a little puzzled. 'Do lions really sunbathe?'

'No, we don't, Charlie; I was joking. I'm waiting for a low flying cheeseburger to pass by.'

I didn't reply straight away. I needed to carefully mull over Daisy's strange reply.

'Do many cheeseburgers fly this way?' I asked after a few moments. I tried to avoid any hint of flippancy in my tone, but it was a ridiculous expectation, so it wasn't easy to avoid a tiny chuckle.

'No. But we all live in the hope of something astoundingly amazing happening in our lives, don't we?'

I was about to say that waiting for a cheeseburger to fly by was an absolutely ludicrous notion, but then I remembered I was having a conversation with a vegetarian lion who could do mental arithmetic….

There was a strangely metaphysical tone in his voice, which I found eerily prescient and slightly unnerving. *My teacher, Mr Pagham-Smythe, often used the term "metaphysical" in lessons, and I quite liked the sound it made, so I used it when I was thinking. But I was not quite ready to use it in a conversation, not just yet.*

It was almost as if Daisy had stretched down into my soul and found a longing desire that I didn't know existed. I would have to be very careful about what I discussed with him in the future. He seemed to have the ability to see things that I couldn't.

'What, for a burger to fly past?' I eventually replied. I thought Daisy wouldn't pick up on my voice's subtle tone of disbelief, but he did.

'Everybody's waiting for something Chas,' replied Daisy in a meandering tone.

'I'm not,' I replied. 'I didn't think I was waiting for anything except my birthday and Christmas.'

'Yes, you are. You're probably waiting for hundreds of things.'

'Like what?' I asked inquisitively.

'Waiting to go back to school tomorrow, to meet some new friends - for your Sunday dinner – for the day when you finish school and get a job – for your first girlfriend... your first kiss, and for me to come down out of this tree and take you out on my boat. And that's just for starters. I could go on all day. You just haven't given it any thought, have you?'

'Not when you put it like that, no,' I replied. I made a note to think more clearly in the future before answering Daisy's questions.

'All I am waiting for is a big juicy cheeseburger to fly past; it's not much to ask, is it?'

After a few moments of quiet reflection, I looked up to where Daisy was lying and muttered, 'I've got one.'

'One what?' asked Daisy with a curiously disinterested expression, not that I could see it. Daisy was still gazing skyward in anticipation...

'Cheeseburger!' I replied, 'I have a cheeseburger.'

'Cheeseburger?' reiterated Daisy, his attention swiftly redirected downwards towards me.

'Yes!'

'For me?' queried Daisy with a tiny hint of uncertainty while removing his sunglasses and glancing down at me. I could see his eyes were wide open with anticipation.

'Yes,' I replied.

There was a flutter of commotion and a crash through the branches as Daisy raced down the tree and landed in front of me.

'Hello Charlie,' said Daisy nicely, now about six inches from my face and gazing longingly into my eyes. He was slowly licking his lips with his enormously long tongue. I instinctively flinched back a few inches.

A very happy Daisy.

'Hello Daisy,' I said.

Daisy's head started searching around for the treat. I took the cheeseburger out of the bag and gave it to him.

Daisy looked so happy.

'It's a bit cold; it's from last night, but....'

'It's wonderful...' said Daisy. 'it's gorgeous and wonderful... thank you so much Charlie.'

I watched as Daisy slowly nibbled away at the burger - carefully savouring and devouring every last little morsel.

After he finished licking his lips, he produced a napkin from somewhere and wiped his mane, which had a few bits of cheese on it. Then he ate the napkin. I was surprised, but then not that surprised.

'Waste not, want not!' mumbled Daisy.

'Right,' I said.

'Okay,' said Daisy, 'let's go down to the boat jetty.'

'Mortimer's bringing me a cup of tea in a minute and a banana for you; shouldn't we wait?'

'No, he won't mind; he'll just think we're playing somewhere in the garden.'

'Okay,' I said, and so we wandered off towards the river.

After about five minutes, we came to another small clearing where some very tall trees were growing. I thought I recognised them.

'What are those?' I asked, pointing up to the top of the trees.

Daisy nonchalantly glanced up, 'coconuts, they're coconuts.'

'Coconuts! But they don't grow in this country.'

'Morti managed it,' replied Daisy smugly.

'Are you sure?' I asked.

Daisy wandered over to one nut that had fallen and picked it up with one paw

Charlie spotted the coconuts.

He presented it to me as if tangible evidence were needed to prove it was what he said it was. 'This…' said Daisy as if to allay any further disbelief while pointing directly at the coconut… 'is a coconut,'

'So it is,' I replied, still puzzled by its very existence. I tapped it a couple of times, 'we could eat this on the boat.'

'We could, but I know what I would prefer,' replied Daisy.

'Sorry, I haven't got another one, maybe next time if I remember.'

Daisy looked intently at me for a moment. 'Is that a promise?'

'I will try the best I can,' I answered.

'Okay.'

Daisy smiled, and we continued walking. We came to a clearing by the river, and I could see the small jetty that Daisy had mentioned. Tied up alongside was an old rowing boat that had once been painted green, but that must have been a long time ago as nearly all the paint had faded away. It was now a horrible yucky colour that, for some inexplicable reason, made me think of death.

I could also see a lot of water in the bottom, so I turned to Daisy.

'That's no use to us; it's sinking; we can't go out in that.'

'Oh ye of little faith,' muttered Daisy. It's not sinking - it's just floating badly; it can be saved.'

'Not sinking, but floating! What's that supposed to mean,' I asked? I was baffled and a little concerned.

That boat is sinking!

'I'm Sorry,' replied Daisy nonchalantly; 'it's a line from my favourite poem. I've always dreamt of using it in a conversation one day, and now, I have. I'm paraphrasing a little, of course.' He was obviously delighted with his achievement. I was confused.

'But it has to make sense; everything has to make sense in the end. That doesn't. There's still loads of water in the bottom,' I replied maddeningly.

Daisy grinned smugly as if he knew how to make sense of it. It was almost as if he knew the answer to everything.

'We will drown if we go out in that!' I exclaimed. I said this very slowly and quite loudly to drive home my point.

'No we won't,' replied Daisy calmly. 'It's only rainwater. We will just have to bail it out before starting our adventure.' Daisy gave me another smug, self-congratulatory smile.

'Oh, I see,' I replied, 'but with what?' I looked around for something to bail out the water, but there was nothing.

Captain Daisy lays back and organises the bailing.

'Give me the coconut you found,' said Daisy.

I handed it over. Daisy took the nut and smashed it against a rock by the side of the jetty. The coconut broke into two pieces. He handed both halves back to me. 'Off you go then.'

'What just me,' I asked?

'I'm the captain,' said Daisy, 'I don't do bailing. I only do the technical and managerial stuff. Bailing is the deck boy's job.' Daisy jumped into the boat and sat back at the far end.

'Where is he?' I asked, glancing around, half expecting somebody else to appear… but no one did.

Daisy pointed at me and smiled, 'you're it, deck boy.'

'Oh,' I replied. I looked despondently at the two halves of the coconut I was holding. This could be a long job.

I glanced pleadingly at Daisy, hoping it might encourage him to help in the bailing, but it didn't work.

'I did bring you a cheeseburger,' I whinged pitifully. It was a pathetically shameful exhibition of awfulness. A hopelessly doomed attempt to negotiate my position on bailing duties. It was unlikely to work, but it was worth a try - anything was worth a try. I gingerly stepped into the boat and started to bail out the water.

'The cheeseburger was your ticket to enter Enigami,' announced Daisy.

'Enigami, what's that?' I asked, sounding a little puzzled.

'It's the world of imagination I live in and the world you can live in if you want.'

'I don't understand,' I replied. I was a little confused.

'You are already there, didn't you realise that?'

'I still don't understand.'

'Do you really think I can talk?' asked Daisy.

Now I was even more confused, 'Yes, of course you can talk. You're talking right now, in case you hadn't noticed.'

Daisy smiled for a few moments.

'I'm a lion, Charlie, a very ordinary lion with no magical powers of speech; the magic is you.'

'But...'

'No but's, that's the truth plain and simple.'

'But you are talking to me,' I made a hand gesture of someone talking and threw a dementedly confused expression at Daisy.

'Charlie, I'm not the special person here... you are,' said Daisy.

'Me?' I replied. I don't understand.'

'Yes, you... You are the innocence of youth, and you are a natural receptor to the world of imagination and all that's in it; that's Enigami. And until you reach a certain age, that's the place you can visit whenever you want to.'

'But how do I stay here?' I was intrigued by Daisy's declaration.

'You just have to stop the world from filling your head with reality for as long as possible. As long as you can do that, you can stay, for a while, in my world.'

'How did I get here?' I asked.

'You do ask a lot of questions,' said Daisy.

'I have to ask questions; I need answers.'

'Ah, but therein lays the paradox,' replied Daisy with a strange, enigmatic smile.

'Paradox,' I repeated curiously, 'what's that?' 'The more questions you ask, the more knowledge you will acquire, and the more knowledge you have, the further away from my world you will be and the less time you have left in Enigami. Information and knowledge fill up the brain. Eventually, you won't have any room left for imagination, and imagination is all you really need in this world. Everything else is just tedious piffle.'

'What's piffle?' I asked. I had never heard that word before.

'It's the rubbish that clogs up your brain if you ask too many questions,' replied Daisy. Too much piffle, and you can become normal because your heads full up with it.'

'But if I don't ask questions, I will be an idiot.'

'No, you won't,' replied Daisy, 'you will find all the answers you need in time. All the knowledge you need in life comes soon enough, and remember, you are never too old to learn something stupid, and never too young to learn something wise, just don't rush it. Think a bit more and say a little less.'

I didn't say anything for a few moments while I processed this insightful scrap of dubious philosophical Daisyspeak. It seemed like a great idea, as I sometimes struggled to remember useless things. So that was it. I just wouldn't bother in future; that seemed like a wonderful way to solve that problem.

'Remember Charlie,' said Daisy adopting a tutorial tone, 'The innocent and the beautiful have no enemy but time. Time is never your friend; it's just something you borrow, and one day you have to give it back.'

'That's awesome,' I replied. 'Did you just make that up?'

'Sort of... with a little help from a friend. He's a poet.'

'He's very clever.'

'And very beautiful,' replied Daisy whimsically.

When the water was all gone, I looked at Daisy and smiled.

'Ship's ready, captain.' I saluted Daisy.

'Right,' said Daisy, 'let's begin our adventure.'

Daisy grabbed hold of the two oars.

'Untie us, Charlie boy,' commanded Daisy

Charlie daydreams while Daisy rows.

'Aye Aye, Captain,' I replied. I cast off the rope that moored us to the jetty, and we started to float away.

Daisy started rowing; he was very good at it.

'Where are we going?'

'Just for a row, we might see some of my friends.'

CHAPTER 6

Noof.

I wondered who Daisy's friends might be. Could they be more talking lions?

'Just sit back and watch me; you will be rowing back, by the way,' said Daisy.

'Oh, I see, right.' I watched Daisy very carefully; it looked easy, but it probably wasn't.

Daisy gently rowed downriver while I laid back, half asleep, trailing my fingers in the water, sending out a thin wake that rippled all the way back to the riverbank. I glanced up at Daisy at the other end, happily rowing away while gazing into the sky, and I thought how strange it was that I was having a boat ride with a wise lion that could not only talk but also knew how to row a boat. I wondered what else I might encounter in the days and weeks ahead. Today was a day like no other day I had ever known.

I heard a loud quacking noise that brought me back from my daydream and glanced up to see half a dozen ducks passing overhead.

'Do you know where they are going?' I enquired.

'Daisy glanced at me for a moment, then looked thoughtfully at the water, then glanced up at the ducks. His expression seemed to indicate that he was contemplating some incredibly complex philosophical theory that would explain all the problems in the world and what the ducks were doing.

'They're flying south for the sun, probably Africa,' he replied after some deliberation. It's in that direction... I think.' Daisy pointed an oar in the same direction the ducks were flying.

Where are they going?

'How do you know these things?' I asked, in total awe of Daisy's knowledge.

'I was born with a compass in my head,' he smartly replied.

'Were you really?' I innocently asked.

'No,' get real, they're flying south because that's the way they're flying, so it must be in that direction, or they would wind up at the North pole, wouldn't they? And that's very cold, so I am told.

'But why?' I continued, immediately realising that I was leaving myself wide open to more ridicule.

'It's warmer in winter. Everybody buggers off in September, well nearly everybody, not me obviously, I can't fly. There is an old Chinese saying about it… "Fly south when nights draw colder, and you will always find red apples in the larder of life."

'What does that mean?' I asked, expecting a profound, meaningful explanation.

'I haven't got a scooby doo,' replied Daisy with complete indifference, 'I just heard it somewhere. It sounded very intellectual and worldly-wise, so I thought I would mention it.'

'But you don't know what it means?' I replied. I must have looked bewildered because I was - a bit.

'Nope,' said Daisy.

'But why say it if you don't know what it means?'

'Because that's what lions do, say odd things.'

'Do they?' I asked.

'Well, I do. I don't actually know about all the other lions. I think it's a bit like African jungle fever, but in the garden.'

'What's that?'

'Well, if you're on your own long enough, you start talking to the trees... any old nonsense.'

'Do you?' I asked.

'Sometimes.'

'Oh,' I replied.

It went quiet for a moment...

'Isn't Africa where lions come from?' I asked.

'Yes,' replied Daisy wistfully, 'I think so.'

'Is that where you came from?'

Daisy kept on rowing and thought about the question.

'My great-great-grandparents came from the sweepingly majestic sun-kissed Savanna grasslands of Kenya in Africa. But I was born here... in the arse end of Hounslow on a wet Wednesday.'

'You shouldn't say arse in front of an innocent child?' I replied, scolding Daisy. I didn't think it was very likely that I would be reprimanded by a lion for swearing.

Daisy looked around, searching for something, 'Child,' he queried?

'Me, I'm the child,' I replied.

'Oh, I see,' Daisy paused for a few moments. 'No, I suppose I shouldn't. But nobody would believe you if you told them, so what the hell.'

I had to smile. 'So, you were born here?'

'Oh yes, on the sweepingly majestic plains of downtown Chiswick. That's the back garden of Number 1 Stanley Road to you and me. It doesn't have quite the same ring, though, does it?'

'No, not really,' I replied. It definitely didn't sound as exotic. It went quiet for another few moments, and Daisy continued rowing up the river… 'It's always sunny in Kenya, you know,' said Daisy wistfully, 'shines every day, so my mum told me. I wouldn't mind going there on holiday.'

The thought of Daisy going on holiday amused me; the idea of him plodding around the jungle wearing sunglasses amused me even more.

'A holiday would be nice,' I said.

'Could be a tiny problem at the airport, though?' muttered Daisy.

'Hmm, maybe,' I replied.

Daisy suddenly produced the sunglasses he had on earlier and put them on again. 'Rayburn Aviators, now I look like Tom Cruise in Top gun - - we could be brothers.

'What do you think?' He threw his head back into a striking pose for a few moments.

'I can hardly tell the difference,' I mumbled while gently biting my tongue.

'Do I look a bit like Tom Cruise? That's the question.'

I was beginning to understand how Daisy's mind worked… a little.

Just then, the boat suddenly lifted up into the air, hovering six feet or so above the water.

'What's happening?' I shouted, lurching over to grab hold of the side of the boat, half expecting to be tipped into the water at any moment.

'All I can see is an enormous bum,' said Charlie

CHAPTER 7

Baggers and Fliss.

'Don't worry, I know what it will be,' replied Daisy nonchalantly. He pulled the oars into the boat.

Fliss (Fliss was a Hippo!) slowly emerged from the water just under the boat. She had tiny sticky-out ears, one with a gold earring and the other with a rose tucked behind it. Her ears looked like large oysters. She had large brown eyes with a sleepy warm, contentedness that couldn't help but make me smile. For a moment, I thought I was dreaming.

Are they really hippo's or am I dreaming?

Then Baggers (another Hippo) suddenly appeared behind us. For some reason, he reminded me of Tom Hanks in Forest Gump, one of my favourite films. Why I thought that at that particular moment, I will never know. It must have been due to the imminent threat of being drowned by a colossal Hippo.

'Hi Daisy,' said Baggers with a long-drawn-out sigh; it was almost as if he didn't have enough energy to talk but was making a special effort just for Daisy, 'how's it going?'

'Hi Baggers,' replied Daisy, a little more chirpily, 'I'm good; how's it going with you?'

'We're good.' Baggers wafted closer to the boat, looking intently at me, squinting his eyes as if he wasn't sure what I was. The boat suddenly dropped down as Fliss disappeared under the water.

'Your lunch appears to be talking to me!' said Baggers.

'Is that your lunch, Daisy?' asked Baggers pulling up alongside the boat.

'No,' replied Daisy. 'He's my friend; I tend not to eat my friends.'

'Oh,' said Baggers disappointedly, 'Fair enough. Probably a bit too bony for lunch anyway; you need a decent bit of meat.'

I gave Baggers a friendly wave in the vain hope that he wouldn't try to eat me.

'He's talking!' I whispered to Daisy. I had been so surprised by their everyday conversation; it had taken me a few moments to realise what was happening.

'We all talk to each other,' replied Daisy in the same casual fashion he always adopted even whenever I thought we were facing disaster,' it's what we do.'

'Your lunch appears to be talking!' exclaimed Baggers, also looking surprised. His eyes opened a little bit wider in amazement.

'Yes, some of the two-legged's are amazingly articulate, aren't they?' replied Daisy smirking at me.

'So, who is your strange-looking inedible friend Daisy? Is he with us or the other lot?'

'He's in our world at the moment; he can hear us, by the way.'

'Oh, sorry, of course, what's his name?'

'My name's Charlie,' I interrupted, 'I am here, you know.' I felt a little peeved, being talked about as if I wasn't. It was beginning to feel a bit like breakfast time.

'Sorry about that; you can never tell,' replied Baggers turning to face me. 'Hello Charlie, nice to meet you.'

'Nice to meet you too,' I replied. 'Are you anything to do with why we're stuck up in the air just now?' I casually asked.

'Sorry about that, it was probably Fliss, doing her yoga. I think you were sitting on top of her bum. She was doing a "downward dog" the last I looked. No need to worry; she could never keep that up for long, especially if you two were sitting on her back.'

'Doing Yoga!' I asked curiously.

'Yes.'

'Hippo's doing yoga?'

'Yes,' replied Baggers nonchalantly as if all hippos did yoga.

'Will she come back?' I enquired gingerly.

Where has Baggers gone?'

'Don't worry, she'll probably be too knackered. You know she's not just any old hippo; that is my wife, and she's well aware that you have to stay slim and attractive for your partner as you get older.' Baggers shrugged with a casual air of swaggering self-gratification.

'Fliss is your wife,' I queried?

'Yes,' replied Baggers before disappearing under the water.

At that, Fliss popped up under the boat again.

'Where has baggers gone?' she asked.

'For a swim, I think,' said Daisy.

I thought we were in danger of falling into the river again, but just at that moment, the boat suddenly plunged back into the water, and Fliss re-emerged to one side.

Charlie waves and smiles nicely at Fliss

Fliss slowly looked up and down the boat, first at Daisy, then at me, then back to Daisy. I waved at Fliss, hoping she wouldn't eat me if I smiled nicely.

'Were you sitting on my bum,' asked Fliss?

'Not exactly,' replied Daisy, 'We were quietly rowing downriver, and your bum popped up underneath us.'

'Oh, I see; I am sorry. Are you both alright?'

'Fine,' said Daisy.

'Me too,' I added.

'It speaks,' exclaimed Fliss. Her eyes opened a little wider with surprise.

'Yes, I do, and I'm Charlie, not an "it" if you don't mind.

'I love cheeseburgers,' rumbled Fliss.

'Sorry, Fliss,' interrupted Daisy, 'I was just explaining to Baggers.

Charlie's in our world at the moment; he's eleven but still a little innocent and naive.'

'Eleven and a half actually,' I corrected

'Eleven and a half then,' said Daisy with a grunt.

'Innocent and naïve, that's a rarity these days,' said Fliss.

'And what's more, he brought me a cheeseburger this morning,' added Daisy.

'Ahh,' said Fliss, 'now I understand why you're taking him out for a boat ride.

Fliss turned to face me and threw an enormous wide-mouthed hippo smile, 'I don't suppose you have another one?'

'What, you like cheeseburgers as well,' I asked, peering deep into Fliss's mouth without making it look too obvious. I had never seen a mouth that big before.

'Doesn't everyone?' replied Fliss.

'I'll try to get you one the next time I come out rowing.'

'Thank you,' replied Fliss.

Turning to Daisy, Fliss asked, 'how's old grumpy Morti?'

'He's okay,' replied Daisy.

'Has he forgiven me yet for our little problem?' asked Fliss.

'Oh yes, he never holds a grudge for long. So where are you two off to?' asked Daisy.

'Thought we would sneak up to the main river and see who's about.'

'That sounds like fun,' said Daisy.

'Thank you,' said Fliss.

Baggers came back to the surface, and a large stork suddenly appeared, fluttering its wings and hovering frantically over the top of him for a few seconds.

'Hi Baggers,' said the stork, eventually settling down on Baggers' shoulder. He started to scrutinise the top of Baggers' head.

'Hi Noof,' said Baggers, 'Are you looking for a snack?'

'If you don't mind,' replied Noof, 'I fancy a nice juicy snail for lunch.'

'I'm sure there are a few of the buggers living up there somewhere.'

'Yep,' replied Noof, waggling a giant snail he had just picked off Baggers's head, 'I've got a nice one.'

He proceeded to turn the snail over and jam it into a small fold of skin on Baggers' back. Once it was secure, he started stabbing the shell with his beak, eventually loosening the snail before gobbling it down in one gulp. After a few seconds, ' Noof burped. 'De….licious,' thank you Baggers .'

Noof dropped in for lunch.

'Anytime,' said Baggers.

'See you tomorrow,' said Noof as he majestically ascended.

'See you,' replied Baggers.

I was utterly mesmerised by what I had just seen. 'Is that normal?' I asked.

'We all help each other out if we can,' replied Baggers, 'it's the only way we will save the planet.'

'Eating snails will save the world?' I enquired, but without any real conviction.

'Everything helps,' replied Baggers.

'Well, I'm sorry,' I continued, 'but the world is doomed to extinction if I have to eat snails. They are horrible.'

'Fair enough,' replied Baggers. The Hippos and the storks can run the world; when you are all gone, we can't do a worse job than your lot, can we?'

I smiled at Baggers and began to consider whether, in years to come, I would look back at these days and wonder if they ever really happened. In the moment, as events unfold, you cannot know what will happen next. History is being created each and every moment as we live. The whole episode of any part of history will always be viewed differently in the future after it has been edited by time to assimilate it into something that we can relate to and understand. Therefore all the strange things happening now may one day be consigned and attributed to the ramblings of an overactive imagination and nothing more. But these things are happening; I know they are.

I awoke from my daydream and looked at Daisy.

Baggers and Fliss were up ahead, slowly waggling their way upriver. Daisy continued rowing behind them, ensuring he didn't get too close.

'How long have they lived here?' I asked.

'Baggers and Fliss?' enquired Daisy, 'I don't know for sure, but it must have been before I was born.'

CHAPTER 8

Estate agents only tell you what they want you to know.

'How come nobody noticed two Hippos?'

'Wow,' I replied, 'I wonder why nobody ever mentioned the hippos?'

'Who would?' asked Daisy, appearing a little intrigued by the question

'Well, I thought the estate agent might have said something.'

'I suppose they might have if they knew about Enigami, but most people don't, and anyway, I'm not sure that mentioning lions and hippos roaming about just beyond your back garden would have been a great selling point.

'Maybe not,' I replied. 'So, what is this Enigami you keep talking about?'

'You could say it's whatever you want it to be,' replied Daisy.

'But where is it?' I asked.

'Charlie,' replied Daisy speaking softly and adopting a serious expression. It was not unlike his teacher Mr Pagham-Smythe when he wanted to explain something quite important, 'you know that your garden doesn't go all the way down to the river?'

'Yes, I thought that was a little strange.'

'Well, that's because none of the houses in Stanley Road go down to the river... except Morti's.'

'Why only Morti's?' I asked, still not fully understanding the significance.

'Well, let me explain,' said Daisy. 'When Henry Stanley, that's Mortimer's Grandfather, bought the house over a hundred years ago, it came with all the land on both sides of the river. But he had to build a wall around all the ground next to the river so his lions couldn't escape. He didn't want them wandering off and eating the residents of Chiswick. That might have upset them a bit.

'I see,' I replied.

'That's why you have a very tall wall at the bottom of your garden. Now Henry wanted to give this area an African sounding name, so he called it Enigami.'

'After Stanley had the lions for a while, he decided to branch out and buy a couple of hippos to live in the river. He was even thinking of getting two chimpanzees at one stage, but I don't think that ever happened.'

'Now I understand,' I replied.

'There is a little more,' said Daisy, 'But I will tell you about that later.'

As they drew closer to the junction with the River Thames, I noticed the river was a lot narrower, and the wall nearly came to the edge on both sides. There was a sandbank at the mouth of the creek, so very few boats could enter or leave.

'I normally stop here, sit on the sandbank, and watch the pleasure boats go by,' said Daisy.

Charlie and Daisy chill on the sandbank.

He jumped out of the boat onto the sandbank and pulled the rowing boat onto the bank. I jumped out, and we both sat down on the sand.

'Can't' they see you?' I asked.

'Most of them are too busy looking at other things, and the rest are probably too drunk to see anything.'

'My dad gets drunk sometimes.'

'I bet he misses a few things when he does,' said Daisy.

'Only what my mum throws at him, and then he always shouts Goal! It makes my mum laugh.'

'So he's a happy drunk?'

'Oh yes. He never seems to be miserable.'

'You're very fortunate.'

'Am I?' I replied.

'Some people get very nasty when they have a drink.'

'Does Morti get drunk?' I asked.

'Sometimes. When he's reminiscing, then he gets tired and emotional and a bit sentimental,' replied Daisy.

'Why?'

'He misses his family.'

'He has a family,' I exclaimed.

'Hello, you two,' interrupted Baggers, suddenly surfacing. Fliss flashed us an enormous smile that I thought was a bit frightening.'

'Where have you been?' asked Daisy.

'We were in the mud having a flap about; it was great fun.' Oddly, Fliss was looking slightly embarrassed. She flicked Baggers a peculiar smile. It was one of those smiles people make when they have a guilty secret they don't really want to share with anybody else.

'Oh, you haven't been having sex again, have you?' asked Daisy bluntly. He could always read Fliss's face.

Fliss threw Daisy a childlike "who, me" type expression.

Daisy flashed Fliss and Baggers a reproachful glare of nausea as she carefully examined their faces for any sign of shame.

'Oooh, that is disgusting; I drink that water,' said Daisy.

An inappropriate conversation.

Stunned by the nature of the conversation, I immediately stuck a finger in each ear and started to sing.

'Nooooo,' said Baggers, 'I wasn't, absolutely not.'

Fliss looked at Baggers with an expression of surprise. 'Well, I was with somebody; I thought it was you. I wonder who it was… they definitely knew how to move the mud.' She looked up in the air with a quizzical expression.

Daisy laughed, 'Move the mud?' He asked with a curious expression. It was all getting a bit out of hand.

'Why is Charlie singing?' asked Baggers, appearing a little intrigued.

'No idea,' said Daisy.

'Have they stopped talking about sex yet?' I asked tentatively, removing my finger out of one ear. I kept my finger very close in case I had to stick it back in again.

'Yes,' said Baggers. 'We will talk about the weather now; that's traditional after having....

'Stop!' I shouted. 'I'm an innocent child. I'm not supposed to hear these things.' I stuck my finger back in my ear and started singing again.

Fliss and Baggers laughed.

'It's alright; we won't mention it again,' said Baggers. He gestured at me to take my fingers out.

I cautiously removed them.

'Why were you singing? Is that what they do in your world?' asked Fliss.

'It's to block out your inappropriate conversation,' I snapped back. I was feeling a little embarrassed.

'Inappropriate conversation? Oh, I see,' replied Fliss. But she didn't. I don't think they understood what that meant, not in their world.

'We should have bought a picnic,' suggested Daisy, 'that would have been nice.'

'Would there be cheeseburgers?' asked Fliss, with a smile and a tiny hint of expectation.

'I could bring some next week,' I suggested.

Daisy looked at me to make sure he would still get one.

'Three cheeseburgers, I won't forget,' I confirmed. Daisy smiled and licked his lips.

'I could bring deckchairs,' I added.

'Not for me,' said Baggers, 'the wood gets stuck in my teeth.'

'To sit on, not to eat.' I explained.

'Oh, sorry,' said Baggers.

'He can be a bit stupid at times,' said Fliss, 'especially after flapping about in the mud.'

I glared at Fliss for a moment, wondering if this would lead the conversation back to somewhere inappropriate, but it didn't.

'Anyway, I have a question.' I thought I would try to change the conversation to another topic.

'Yes, said Daisy.'

'How come you all like cheeseburgers? You can't exactly pop down the road to Mackie D's without causing a bit of an issue.'

'Silly boy,' said Daisy, haven't you heard of Uba Eats? They deliver.'

'But you can't order them, they can't hear you, and how would you pay? You can't possibly have a credit card.'

'No, you're right, we can't. But Nancy used to buy them for us.'

'Nancy?' I repeated inquisitively, 'who is Nancy?'

'Morti's daughter,' said Daisy.

'He has a daughter?' I asked, sounding surprised.

'Morti must have gone for a flap in the mud,' said Baggers, 'that usually does it for us.'

Fliss glared at Baggers.

Baggers stopped talking.

'And a wife,' continued Daisy in a sensible tone, 'Eleanor was her name. She was here for years, then one day Nancy popped up, about ten years ago, as I remember.'

'But they don't live here anymore?' I asked.

'No.'

'Where did they go?'

'I don't know. They were here, then one day they just disappeared.'

'Wasn't that a little strange?'

'Maybe, maybe not,' said Daisy thoughtfully, 'my mum was here for years, and then one day she wasn't. I never knew where she went. I thought maybe she'd gone down to the river for a swim and was swept away, but who knows what happens to us when we disappear.'

I felt a little sad hearing Daisy's poignant recollection of his mum.

I had a good idea about what had probably happened to her, but I

didn't want to mention it just in case it upset him.

My Uncle Bert had disappeared just before we moved to Stanley Road, and dad had been very despondent for a couple of weeks. I think he missed him quite a bit.

So I knew how it might affect Daisy if I mentioned what I thought had probably happened. I remembered reading somewhere that Lions lived for about thirty years, which wasn't long compared to Bert, who was nearly fifty years old when he disappeared.

'Maybe you should ask Morti where his wife and Nancy went,' said Fliss glancing oddly in my direction.

Fliss had been quietly listening to the conversation.

'I don't know if that's a good idea,' said Daisy, 'that might upset Morti, and he may not let you come round anymore.'

'And we won't get our cheeseburgers,' mumbled Baggers.

'Maybe I won't mention it yet unless it comes up in conversation,' I replied.

'Sounds like the best idea,' said Daisy.

The sun was surprisingly warm for this time of year, and I leaned back on the ground and closed my eyes. Daisy sat on the grass and nodded off to sleep. Baggers and Fliss paddled around in the mud on the side of the river, gently splashing each other before eventually closing their eyes and having a snooze. There were lots of funny grunts and snorts as they slept.

After about an hour, I woke up and prodded Daisy to wake him.

'We should be getting back soon. Morti will wonder where we are, and my mum will be expecting me back for Sunday dinner.'

'Okay,' said Daisy stretching out before wandering back to the boat.

'We're going now,' said Daisy, but Baggers and Fliss were fast asleep and couldn't hear him.

'They've worn themselves out,' said Daisy clambering into the boat.

'Hmm,' I replied.

Daisy having a rest and catching a few rays.

'I started rowing back to the jetty at the end of Morti's garden. Daisy sat back, put his sunglasses on and dozed, and I mulled over all the things we had talked about today. There were a few sad things, which I wasn't expecting, but then I didn't really know what to expect.

I would like to know what happened to Eleanor and Nancy, but I wouldn't mention it just yet, remembering Daisy's advice on the matter. I would leave that for another day. Morti might even mention it.

We arrived back at the jetty and jumped out. I tied up the boat, and we slowly wandered back up the pathway to the house.

'So, did you enjoy meeting Baggers and Fliss today?' asked Daisy

'Yes,' I replied. They were funny, and Noof made me laugh, picking the snail off Baggers's head and eating it. That really cracked me up.'

I paused for a moment, 'I was sorry to hear about your mum disappearing,' oddly, I felt awkward about using the "died" word, so I didn't. I wasn't sure if Daisy had realised that she was probably dead. Death was different for Daisy, but I wasn't quite sure how. Maybe it was different for animals; perhaps they had already come to terms with their own mortality. More than I had. It was a different world, after all.

'Maisy was a good mother, and Muriel was a good dad,' said Daisy. I miss them both. He turned to glance at me and smiled.

'Are your mum and dad good people?'

Good people, I thought, that was a strange question. 'Yes, they are. They love each other, and my sister Mags and me.'

'Good,' said Daisy. That's all that really matters.

We arrived back at the patch of short grass where Mortimer was asleep in a deckchair.

'Will I see you next weekend?' I asked.

'Can't you come before?' said Daisy.

'No, not during the week, I have to go to school Monday till Friday, so I can't. I will have homework to do as well.'

'Does that mean you are acquiring more knowledge' asked Daisy warily?

'Some,' I replied.

'Don't learn too much, too soon, will you?'

'Why not?' I asked.

'I told you yesterday, don't you remember?'

'About getting too much knowledge and losing you?'

'Yes.'

'That can't really happen, can it?'

'Charlie, I told you at the beginning, the more knowledge you get, the less time you will be able to spend with us.'

'Oh… I see.'

'That's the way it is. I can't do anything about it,' added Daisy.

'I will remember,' I confirmed.

'Good. I will miss you when you do leave us,' said Daisy.

'I will try not to become clever too quickly,' I replied.

'Excellent,' said Daisy with a large grin. She was obviously pleased with the arrangement.

'You will be clever soon enough, then you will have to leave Enigami forever because you will be intelligent but ordinary.'

'And nobody likes to be ordinary, do they?' I replied with a grin.

'Absolutely not,' said Daisy.

I wandered off, saying a quiet goodbye to Morti before I left. Daisy waved a paw before I disappeared into the house.

'See you tomorrow, Daisy,' said Charlie

CHAPTER 9

The trouble with lies.

Me and dad having a chat.

'So...' said dad sitting in his armchair, reading his newspaper and smoking his pipe. I never quite understood what the pipe thing was all about. I watched him as he stuffed the bowl with tobacco and then set fire to it. There was a lot of sucking involved and a lot of smoke, but that appeared to be it. It was a mystery, but remembering what Daisy had told me, I decided not to ask any questions about it, as it was probably not essential. That would be another small part of my brain not being filled with unnecessary useless information.

'… what do you do when you go to Mortimer's,' continued dad?

'I play football with Daisy… his cat.'

'Football?' replied dad with a curious tone in his voice.

'You don't play football with Mortimer then?'

'No, he's much too old. He must be nearly a hundred.'

Dad lowered the newspaper he was reading so he could see me.

'Are you sure?'

'Yes,' I replied confidently.

'How old do you think I am?' he asked.

'Not that old; you haven't got a beard.'

'I would say he was around about fifty,' said dad, and I am forty-four.'

'Oh,' I replied, 'maybe I was wrong then.'

'I think so, a little bit,' said dad. 'the beard makes him look much older.'

'So, not a hundred?' I asked.

'No, I don't think so. So is Daisy a large cat? She must be quite big to push a ball around?'

'He's quite big.' I replied gingerly, 'and she's a he, by the way.'

'A he?' repeated dad, sounding confused, 'but you called him Daisy.'

'I know, but that's Daisy's name.'

'Oh,' replied dad. Appearing understandably bewildered by the odd arrangement, 'isn't that a little strange?'

'No, not really, all things considered.'

'Oh,' said dad. He seemed reluctant to continue with that line of enquiry, and I thought it was best not to elaborate any further. Any specific details about Daisy - might cause some alarm for mum and dad. I would just stick to a vague outline for now.

'Isn't it a bit strange playing football with a cat?' queried Mum after a few moments. She was still doing the ironing.

'It's only a small ball; Daisy couldn't play with a normal ball.'

That's the trouble with lies; they can quickly get out of control and go a bit silly once you've started.

'Does Daisy play in goal?' asked dad

'Sometimes.'

'Is he any good?'

'He's alright; he even stops the ball sometimes if he sees it.'

'You should ask him to go for a trial at Chelsea football club. They need a goalie who can see the ball.' Dad laughed at his own joke, then lifted his newspaper and continued reading. Mum and I watched him sniggering away behind his newspaper; we could see the paper shaking. Dad's giggling was interspersed with the occasional cloud of smoke breaking loose from his pipe and appearing just above his head. I glanced at mum, and she smiled at me as if to say, "don't say anything; he'll only get upset and go into a huff."

That was it. Interrogation over for the day.

CHAPTER 10

'Too much knowledge and my brain will be
overfull....'

'Can I come and meet Daisy?' asked Mags.

The following day, I ate porridge with honey for breakfast, and Mags had toast and marmalade. I told mum and dad I was going to play with Daisy next door.

'Have you done your homework?' asked Mum.

'Yes, all done, and I've tidied my room.'

'Thank you,' said mum, sounding a little surprised.

'Can I come round and meet Daisy?' asked Mags.

I had been expecting this at some point, and obviously, I was a little concerned about what she might say when she first saw Daisy.

'Not today,' said mum. 'I want you to give me a hand making a cake for tea.' I breathed a sigh of relief.

'Okay,' said Mags reluctantly.

'I will have to come round some other time Charlie,' said Mags.

'No problem,' I replied, 'see you later, mum,' and off I went.

'Be back for tea,' said mum.

'Okay.'

'Goodbye, dad.'

'Bye, son, see you later.' I couldn't see dad. He was still hiding behind his newspaper, but I could see another cloud of smoke slowly drifting across the room.

....

I banged on Mortimer's door and waited. The door eventually opened. I wondered why it took so long, but then I thought maybe I shouldn't worry about how long it takes; it didn't really matter, as Daisy would say.

'Hello, Mortimer,' it still seemed odd calling him by his first name.

'Hello Charlie, I suppose you want to come in and play with Daisy?'

'Yes, please, if you don't mind.'

'Not at all. I think he missed you this week. Do come in.'

I wandered through to the kitchen and then turned back to face Morti for a moment.

'Did Daisy say something?' I asked the question before remembering Morti didn't know Daisy could talk.

'No, he didn't say anything… it was just a feeling.'

'Oh,' I said, relieved that I hadn't let the cat out of the bag.

'He has been moping around a bit. He's like that when he's unhappy about something.'

Mortimer looked at me for a few moments. I could see he was carefully thinking about what he was going to say next.

'I used to talk to his dad, Muriel.'

'You spoke to Muriel?' I wasn't sure how I should respond to that.

'Well, I think I did,' continued Morti, 'But sometimes, I wonder if maybe I just imagined it. It seemed so natural at the time but then talking to a lion is a little unusual.

'That must have been quite a few years ago,'

'Yes, it was,' replied Morti, 'when I was around your age… but it all seemed to stop after I started grammar school.'

'Grammar school,' I queried, 'What's that?' I half expected it to be a special school where you had to go to learn where to put commas and full stops in sentences. It didn't sound like much fun.

'That's where children used to go after passing school exams when you were eleven years old - if you were lucky. Only the clever children went to grammar school; the rest went to secondary school. Unfortunately, I was quite clever, which is why Muriel couldn't talk to me anymore.'

'Why?' I queried.

'Hasn't Daisy told you?' said Morti in a matter of fact way. He smiled as if he knew something I didn't. 'You do know he can converse, don't you?'

'Converse?' I queried. I wasn't sure what that meant.

'Speak: he can talk to you,' clarified Morti with a smile that came from far away and long ago.

'Yes.' I replied gingerly, feeling strangely embarrassed with my admission. It could have been a trick question for all I knew, but then Morti didn't usually do trick questions.

I could be going mad; that was a distinct possibility. At one stage, I did imagine that the whole encounter the previous weekend had been a drug-induced illusion. But as I hadn't taken any psychotropic drugs recently… (I had never taken any drugs except Calpol when I was about five years old, which my mum gave me whenever I had a toothache.)… and I didn't really know what a drug-induced illusion was, it was just something one of my friends at my old school had mentioned. His parents did take drugs from time to time and went a bit funny in the head.

So, I had ruled out that possibility. Whatever had happened definitely happened.

'It's okay, I do understand,' said Morti.

'Has he never spoken to you,' I asked warily? What concerns I did have were slowly fading away.

'Never,' replied Morti. Unfortunately. I had gotten too much knowledge by the time Daisy was born. But you are still innocent and perhaps a little naïve. Your head's not full of arcane rubbish yet - so I presumed he might have spoken to you.'

'I'm not an empty-headed idiot,' I exclaimed a little hastily, taking offence at something that, looking back, I realise wasn't offensive or insulting at all. I had simply misunderstood Morti's explanation. I wondered what arcane meant.

'Being young means you are genetically temperamental, occasionally unstable and sometimes volatile in the face of unwarranted criticism,' replied Morti smiling. 'I'm sorry. I wasn't saying you were an idiot; it's nothing to do with that.' It's about the innocence of youth and your receptive accessibility.'

I wasn't sure what that meant. I could feel my eyebrows spontaneously pinching together and my eyes squinting in bewilderment. Morti could obviously see I was struggling to understand.

'It's how approachable your mind is to the world of imagination,' said Morti.

'Is that good or bad?' I asked.

'It's good, believe me, it's really good. I wish I could be like you are now. Enigami is a wonderful world while it lasts.'

'You've been there!' I exclaimed. I was surprised.

'Yes, I escaped from this world for a short while, but it was many years ago,' confirmed Morti.

'It's all rather peculiar, isn't it?' I asked.

'Yes,' replied Morti, 'it is, but it's also magical in an odd way,' It protects you from insecurity and vulnerability to uncertainty. But as you grow older, these things don't affect you quite so much, they don't seem to matter anymore, but they do matter; you just don't feel it any longer. You become strong and more resilient… but as you become stronger, your innocence is sacrificed. And one day, it's completely gone like a puff of smoke, and you realise you can't go back there anymore. That's when you begin to wonder if it ever really existed at all.'

'It does exist; I been there,' I excitedly replied. I felt the urgent desire to reassure Morti and alleviate any doubts he might still have about what he could remember.

'Can I ask you a personal question?' I ventured a little cagily. I had already discussed the subject with Daisy the previous weekend, but he hadn't exactly answered my question, and it still bothered me. Mum always said I asked too many awkward questions for someone so young.

'Of course,' replied Morti, 'anything.'

I cautiously proceeded… 'Daisy mentioned your wife Eleanor and your daughter Nancy.'

I did wonder why Morti seemed so sad all the time.

Morti went quiet for a moment and sat down in his old armchair. He looked at me with his head tilted to one side as if he were looking for something.

Then Morti's head came back to an upright position, and he replied.

'Did he?'

'Yes.'

'And what did Daisy say?'

'Only that that they were here for a long time and then one day they weren't.'

Morti thought about what I had just said for a moment before answering. I couldn't tell whether he was conjuring up a story that would end any speculation I might have or if he was deciding how to tell me the truth. I suppose it all depended on whether he thought I was old enough to understand the truth.

'Did Daisy ever speak to Nancy?' asked Mortimer. I could see this was not easy for him, and I began to wish I hadn't started the conversation.

'Yes, he did.'

'What did Nancy say?'

'Daisy didn't say, just that they were good friends.'

Morti didn't say anything for a moment...

'I don't know where they went. I came home one day, and Eleanor had packed all of her things and some of Nancy's, and they were gone.'

'Oh.' I didn't know what to say.

'She left me a note to say they were going far away and begged me not to try to find them... so I didn't.'

'I did think about it many times, but what would be the point? She had obviously made up her mind, and she must have been thinking about it for a long time, so...'

'Did you love her?' I asked the question before realising how impertinent that was. I don't know what made me ask at that particular moment. I couldn't do anything about Morti's situation, and asking that question wouldn't make a blind bit of difference. Neither would knowing the answer.

Morti looked surprised. 'Yes, I did, both of them, very much; why do you ask?' I could tell he was thinking about them.

'I don't know to be honest. I'm sorry. I'm not old enough to ask that sort of question.'

'Oh, I think you are. You are more mature than you think. It's a relevant and important question, probably the most important one anyone could have asked, but strangely nobody else ever did.'

'Tell me to shut up if I say something offensive or impolite but did your wife love you?' I was really pushing my luck now.

Mortimer looked even more surprised by this question.

I was surprised by the question; I didn't know where they were coming from.

'I thought she did, I thought they both did, but then she left, so obviously I was wrong.'

'Maybe,' I hesitated for a few moments before continuing, I seemed to have morphed into some sort of marriage counsellor, which was a bit worrying, 'maybe she left for another reason?'

'Yes, the police said that when I reported them missing.'

'But they didn't get anywhere?'

'No. Initially, the police did think I had killed both of them. They didn't say as much, but they did have a good look around the house and the garden.'

'Did they say anything about Daisy?' I asked.

'Strangely no. I think he hid up a tree somewhere. Daisy's quite good at that. They wouldn't have been able to see him anyway.'

'What about Baggers and Fliss?'

'Ah, the gay hippos, you've met them?' asked Morti.

'Gay?' I exclaimed, that took me by surprise.'

'You're not homophobic, are you? asked Morti with a curiously guarded expression.

'What's homophobic?' I asked.

'It's when one person can't see how other people can be different yet perfectly normal.

'No, I'm not, but I thought Fliss was a lady hippo.'

'No, Fliss pretends to be, but he's not. His real name is Arthur.

'Oh.' I felt a little confused, 'yes, they were good fun.'

'I think Daisy told them to keep their heads down for a while when the police turned up.'

'They're good at that,' I remarked.

'So, does that address your concerns?' asked Morti.

'I had no concerns for me, just for you; Daisy said it has affected you badly since they disappeared.'

'It has, but life goes on.'

'I can't imagine what life would be like if my mum and Mags disappeared one day without saying a word.'

'It is hard to get your head around something like that,' replied Morti, 'but hopefully, it won't happen to you. It's not very likely, statistically speaking.'

It went quiet for a few moments; I felt a little awkward, 'I'll go and find Daisy then.'

'Yes, you'd better,' said Morti. 'He will be wondering where you are.'

CHAPTER 11

Daisy, the reluctant vegetarian.

I wandered off to the patch of grass in the garden where Daisy usually sat. He was laid on the ground, half-asleep when I arrived.

'Hi, Daisy.'

Daisy opened one eye to see who was speaking.

'Hi Charlie, how have you been?' He opened his other eye and smiled.

'Good, I've been good.'

I sat down in Morti's deckchair and looked at Daisy. Daisy looked back with a suspicious expression.

Daisy looked at me with just a little apprehension.

'Yes,' said Daisy.

'I didn't say anything,' I replied, a little surprised.

'No, but you're going to; I can see that much.'

'Well….'

'Oh dear, here we go,' said Daisy.

'Well, it's all very good, us being able to talk to each other, but I think we should be able to use that to help Morti.'

'He's okay. Most days, I see him when he brings out my lovely Veg-Jet-Tar-Rian lunch.' Daisy broke the word into four tiny pieces, emphasising his utter displeasure. 'It's usually sprouts and something.'

'Being a vegetarian is good for you. It keeps you healthy and helps stop the planet's pollution,' I replied.

Daisy has a sprout and chip issue.

'I don't like sprouts, they make me fart, and when I fart, everybody knows about it. That is definitely polluting the planet.'

'Who's everybody,' I asked?

'Well, Baggers, Fliss, Noof and Morti and now you.'

'I thought you would know loads of people, well, other animals anyway?'

'Not when I fart, I don't. No one wants to know me.'

'Oh, I see. Well, perhaps I could mention that to Morti. I have told him we talk to each other.'

'Was that a good idea?' asked Daisy.

'To be honest, Morti sort of guessed.'

Daisy mused over that for a moment.

'So, how do you want to help Morti?' asked Daisy with a curious expression. It was as if he already knew that whatever it was, it would be a problem.

'It's to do with Eleanor and Nancy and their disappearance.'

'Oh, that,' mumbled Daisy with noticeable reservation.

'It's just a little odd, don't you think, that they should just get up one day, pack their bags, walk out the door and disappear into thin air?'

'I don't know. It's a constant source of amusement to me what two-legged's do,' said Daisy.

'The police thought he might have murdered both of them and buried them in the garden.'

'Well, I never noticed Morti digging up the garden, except once when he planted a few potatoes. But I dug them up and snaffled them when I got hungry one day, so he didn't bother anymore. He did grumble a bit to himself about that, he couldn't understand where they had gone, and obviously, I couldn't tell him. I never did understand why he was planting perfectly edible potatoes in the garden anyway. It's one of those odd things that your people do.'

'So, will you help me?' I asked. I don't know the first thing about investigating a mystery.'

'What, and you think I'm Sherlock Holmes?'

'No, I don't, but there must be something you and the Hippo guys can do. There has to be an advantage - you being able to speak?'

'Well, I haven't worked it out yet, a part that is from being able to ask you for a cheeseburger, which is a definite bonus for me.'

'Don't you know anything at all about what happened to them?'

'Well, I heard the police talking to Morti about two or three weeks after they went missing. From what I could make out, Eleanor may have spoken to the police before she left, but that was it.'

'He could have chopped them up into little pieces and fed them to you, of course. You do like a meaty cheeseburger.'

'Oh, nice thought,' said Daisy, 'I'm beginning to see a rather unpleasant side to you. To start with, that would be a lot of burgers, and there would also be a lot of broken bones. It would be yuck.' Daisy scrunched up his face in disgust at the idea.

'I was only saying.'

'Well, don't. It's horrible. Think nice thoughts... please.'

So you think they are alive?'

'Absolutely.'

'Then we should talk to the police.'

Daisy scrunched up his face again, apparently dumbfounded by my suggestion.

'Talk to the police!' exclaimed Daisy.

'Yes.'

'What, you an eleven-year-old boy who has just moved in next door and hardly knows Morti, or me, a twenty-six-year-old invisible African farting lion who can only talk to children.

Who do you think should speak to the police? Answers on a postcard, please.'

'What's a postcard?' I asked.

'Oh, never mind. It's a turn of phrase.'

'What's that?'

Daisy looked at me in astonishment. 'You don't get out much, do you?'

'I do. I get out most days.'

'That's not quite what I meant,' replied Daisy.

'What did you mean then?'

'When someone asks a question, and there are only two stupid answers available, what you say is… "Answers on a postcard, please." It's a turn of phrase.'

'Like a glib remark?

'Yes, now you're getting it.'

'And "you don't get out much, do you." What does that mean?'

Daisy's head fell forward in frustration… 'It means… you don't seem to know very much, and you must have had a very sheltered life.

'Oh, I see,' I replied, 'Am I a bit dim then?' I was beginning to think I was.

'No, you're not dim; you're just innocent; there's nothing wrong with that.' Daisy smiled.

'I will go into the police station and ask them.'

'They won't tell you anything,' said Daisy.

'I can only try.'

'I can come with you if you like,' said Daisy.

'Now that would be silly. You will frighten everybody if they see you plodding up the road with me.'

'They won't be frightened. They can't see me.'

'Oh,' and where exactly are you going to hide,' I answered a little flippantly, 'in a Tesco carrier bag?'

'I don't have to hide in a bag,' replied Daisy with a hoity-toity expression. No one can see me except children like you and Morti.'

'That sounds a bit farfetched to me despite everything else,' I replied, 'Have you been eating magic mushrooms again? They're making you delusional.' Extracting the urine was becoming a recurring theme in our relationship.

'No, I haven't been eating mushrooms, and I am not delusional as you so nicely put it, thank you,' replied Daisy throwing his head up in the air - taking offence at the slur.

'So how come nobody can see you? Don't tell me; you've got an invisibility cloak; I saw that film.'

'No, I haven't. It's an 'African witch doctors enchantment.'

'A what?' I exclaimed.

'It's an enchantment. When Morti's grandad was in Africa, he met Doctor Livingstone. They were friends for a while. And while they were there, they met an African witch doctor whose daughter was gravely ill with malaria. Now doctor Livingstone gave her some quinine, and she recovered. The witch doctor was so grateful he asked Stanley and Livingstone what he could give them as a reward.'

'Stanley said he wanted to take some animals back home to England and keep them in his garden, but if anybody saw them roaming freely, it could be a problem, so did he have any ideas. The witch doctor suggested he make the animals invisible to everybody except Stanley and young children. Stanley didn't believe he could do it, but he did. And strangely, the enchantment has continued to work ever since....'

CHAPTER 12

Charlie and Daisy visit the Police Station.

So Daisy and I wandered off to the police station on the high street.

When we arrived, I asked to speak to somebody about a missing person. Daisy sat down beside me, picking his toenails and flicking the bits in the air.

'Don't do that,' I said. 'It's disgusting.'

Daisy grunted.

'Excuse me,' said the police officer behind the counter.

'Sorry,' I replied, 'I was just talking to myself.'

'Oh,' replied the officer flashing me a curious smile.

'Can you wait here for a minute? I need to speak to somebody about this.' He wandered off and left us alone.

After about fifteen minutes, another police officer, not in uniform, came out to see me.

'Hello young man,' he spoke in a friendly if slightly condescending manner, 'I'm Inspector Smutherly CID; how can I help you?' For a second, his attention was diverted as he squinted suspiciously at the extensive pile of toe clippings now accumulated in a heap on the floor. He quickly scanned the room searching for a possible miscreant responsible for the nail debris. But there was nobody else there. His attention came back to me - briefly checking that I had socks and shoes on, which I had. He warily continued.

'I understand someone has gone missing?'

'Yes. I am concerned about my neighbour. His wife and daughter have been missing for a while.'

'That's a little strange,' said Inspector Smutherly.

'Have they now,' asked Inspector Smutherly in a carefully measured tone. He spoke with a reassuringly soft welsh accent which put me a little at ease, but I could also see that he was not taking it too seriously. It was as if he were talking to me but dreaming about his favourite fish pie that he would be having for tea.

'So, who exactly are you?' he asked.

'I'm Charles Christmas, but everybody calls me Charlie. I live at number Three Stanley Road in Chiswick, and my neighbour lives at
    number One.'

'Christmas, that's an unusual surname,' said the Inspector.

'Yes, people do mention that,' I replied.

'Not born on the twenty-fifth of December, by any chance, were you? There was a distinct hint of disbelief in his tone. I was used to that by now.

'No, 23rd September actually,' I promptly replied, 'Why?' asking *why* invariably threw people off balance.

'No reason, I just wondered. So you live next door to Mr Mortimer Stanley?'

'Yes. And it's his wife and daughter that have gone missing.'

'Can you wait here for a moment?' he asked politely.

'Yes, of course.'

He wandered off in the same direction as the other officer.

After another fifteen minutes, a third police officer, also not in a uniform, came out. By now, the collection of toenails on the floor had grown considerably.

'Hello, Mr Christmas, I'm Chief inspector Ruddleslip.' He looked at the pile of toenails in the middle of the floor first. 'Did you see where they came from,' he asked with a curious expression while pointing at the clippings.'

'They were here when I arrived,' I answered innocently. Well, they were, in a manner of speaking, only they were attached to Daisy back then.

'Hmm,' he replied, 'very odd. So, I understand you are enquiring about the missing mother and daughter Eleanor and Nancy Stanley?'

'Yes.' I am very concerned for my neighbour, Mr Stanley, as nothing seems to have been done to find them.'

'Is that so,' he replied a little briskly.

'I don't know, for sure, but Mr Stanley has heard nothing, and I was just wondering if you had any news.'

'And why are you asking?'

At that moment, another toe clipping landed on the floor, and I glared at Daisy, who just smirked back. Fortunately, the inspector didn't see it land.

'Well,' I continued, 'I live next door with my mum and dad and my sister Mags. We've just moved in.'

'Yes,' said Chief Inspector Ruddleslip, 'my inspector mentioned that.'

'Well, the other day, I was talking to Mr Stanley, and he mentioned that they disappeared suddenly some time ago, and he didn't know what had happened to them, and he was still very concerned. As we had just moved in, I thought I could do the neighbourly thing and help him by asking you if you knew where they were, that was all.' It was all a bit rambling, and I could see that he thought I was sticking my nose into someone else's business but…

'Oh. I see.' He paused for a minute.

'There isn't much I can tell you, but what I can say, which is the same as we told Mr Stanley, is that they are safe and well. It isn't much, but that's all there is.'

I had an inkling that he knew more than he was telling me, but then he hadn't actually told me anything, so I didn't need to be a rocket scientist to work that one out.

'Oh,' I replied, a little confused by what he had said, 'that doesn't make any sense, though.'

At that, Daisy chipped in. 'I think what he is trying to say is Mrs Stanley has done a runner with another bloke. It's a code the old bill use; it's called copper's lingo.'

'Copper's lingo?' I repeated, never having heard the term before. I knew I should get out more…

'Sorry, I didn't quite catch that,' said the chief inspector, not realising I was talking to Daisy.

I snapped at Daisy, 'Be quiet; you're confusing me,'

'What?' queried the chief inspector, who was taken aback by me apparently telling him to be quiet. (I was talking to Daisy)

'I'm sorry,' what I meant to say was, thank you. Now I understand, I think.' It was becoming very complicated with Daisy constantly sticking his nose in.

'Good,' said the chief inspector. 'I'm glad that's cleared up. Is there anything else I can help you with?'

'Could you tell me where they are living?'

'No. Not really. That's confidential. Mrs Stanley specifically requested that we didn't release those details to anybody.'

'Oh, I see. Well, thank you for your help.'

'No problem, any time.' Is there anything else I can help you with?'

'Err, no,' I replied.

Daisy glanced at me. 'Well, that didn't get us anywhere.'

'You weren't much help, flicking toenails everywhere,' I replied.

'I'm sorry,' said the chief inspector indignantly, obviously taking some offence, 'they aren't my toenails.'

'I'm sorry,' I replied, 'I didn't mean you. I was just talking to myself.'

'Were you?' He looked at me with a suspicious glare.

'Yes.' I replied.

'Um,' he replied.

He smiled briefly and went back into his office, but not before whispering something to another police officer behind the counter and pointing to the large pile of toenail clippings in the middle of the floor.

I left the police station, and Daisy strolled on along behind.

I was no better off than before, but at least I knew they were alive, somewhere.

'So what do we do now?' mumbled Daisy as we wandered up the road.

Someone shouted, and I turned around. A policewoman was running towards us.

I thought she was going to arrest me for the pile of toenails that Daisy had left behind, so I held my hands up for her to clamp on the handcuffs.

I thought I was off to prison again.

She looked at me a little strangely but took no notice of my waving hands. She shook her head. Obviously, I had confused her.

'Hello,' she said, still looking a little confused. 'Are you the one who was just inquiring about the Stanleys?'

'Yes,' I replied.

'Well, I'm not supposed to say anything, but we all thought it was a bit odd, so I thought I should tell you that Eleanor Stanley and her daughter were travelling upriver to somewhere outside of Oxford; they are living on a canal boat she bought.'

'Oh,' I replied. I was a little surprised. 'Well, thank you for that. We will have to see if we can find them. I'm sure that would make Mr Stanley happy. He's very sad at the moment?'

'We?' she queried?

'Sorry, I meant me, I. I will have to try to find them and speak to them.' It was a little confusing with Daisy staring at me.

'She seemed like a nice lady,' continued the policewoman, and her daughter seemed very amicable, just a little odd. I remember from the conversation she had with the inspector that they both missed Mr Stanley terribly, but for some reason, they couldn't go back. It was all rather strange.'

'Well, thank you for that,' I said, 'It could help.'

'I hope it does,' she replied with a smile. Then she turned and started walking back towards the police station before turning back one last time. 'The canal boat that Eleanor and Nancy are living on....'

'Yes!' I interrupted a little impatiently.

'She bought it around here somewhere. Nancy told me all about it while her mother spoke with the chief inspector.'

'Oh,' I said, 'well, that's something to go on.'

'It was called Pink Flamingo, as I remember. It had been painted various shades of pink. That's why they liked the boat so much. That might make it easier for you to find them.'

'Yes, it will. Thank you,' I replied, 'but why are you being so helpful when the chief inspector refused to tell us anything?'

'I think he's wrong. Mrs Stanley and Nancy didn't have a bad word to say about Mr Stanley, so it didn't make any sense for them to leave without a word. There has to be something more to it than that. I just don't know what that is.'

'Thank you,' I said again, 'thank you very much.'

'I do hope it helps you, but please don't say anything about me telling you I would get into trouble.'

'No, of course not,' I replied.

She turned around and continued walking back to the station. I never saw her again.

After a few moments, Daisy turned to me, 'We will have to go to Oxford to investigate the matter further.'

'We?' I replied with a curious glance at Daisy.

'Well, I am your assistant now, aren't I?' We are like private detectives, aren't we?' Daisy paused, 'a bit like Stanley and Livingstone?'

'They weren't private detectives! They were African explorers!'

'But they did find each other… in a huge jungle, so they were a little bit like detectives.'

I was lost for words for a moment. Daisy's logic had me beaten. Sometimes he really confused me.

CHAPTER 13

The Charlie Christmas Private Investigation Agency.

'The Daisy and Charlie Detective Agency, that sounds good,' suggested Daisy as we wandered back home from the police station.

'The Charlie Christmas Private Investigation Agency sounds better,' I swiftly replied.

'Where am I in that?' asked Daisy.

'You can be my assistant. In charge of… making the tea.'

What was that?

Daisy flashed me a mischievous smile as he accidentally walked into an unsuspecting pedestrian, nearly knocking him into the road. The man couldn't fathom out what had just happened, so he continued walking in the opposite direction but kept looking back, half expecting to see something suddenly materialise, but of course, nothing did.

'It's easy being a private eye,' said Daisy.

'Is that what you think?' I asked.

'I've seen a couple of detective series on the TV,' said Daisy, 'so I know what to do.'

'Do you really?'

'Yes. And I am invisible to most people, so that has to be an advantage if I'm working undercover,' replied Daisy with a smug expression.

'Um…' I replied, conceding that Daisy was probably right in that respect. 'Do you actually believe what happens in television detective stories really happens?'

'Yes,' replied Daisy firmly, without the slightest hint of doubt.

'You shouldn't watch TV; it's confusing you,' I replied. 'You should just run around the garden, make a few growling noises, climb a tree occasionally, and sleep all day. Oh, and eat your vegetarian dinner when it arrives. That's what "normal" lions do.' I emphasised the "normal." I couldn't help but snigger.

Daisy was visibly deflated by that put-down. 'That is the most condescending, patronising, demeaning thing anybody has ever said to me.'

I could see that I had upset him a little, so I apologised.

'I'm sorry, but that's the truth of the matter. *You should get out more.* Then you'd know what it's like to live in the real world, not this Enigami wonderland you inhabit.'

I had to smile when I said, *"you should get out more."* I had been waiting to use the expression ever since Daisy had explained it to me.

Daisy scowled. 'We both live here,' corrected Daisy after a few moments, adopting a smug, sanctimonious expression and emphasizing *"both*."

'Both...!' I exclaimed. I'm not delusional.'

'You must be a little bit,' replied Daisy.

'Why?' I snapped.

'You are having a conversation with an invisible lion who cuts his own toenails, in case you forgot.' Daisy glared at me again with a big cheeky smile, 'so, I'm not just any old normal lion.' In fact, calling me normal could almost be considered species discrimination, even bigoted. I am not normal, whatever that is supposed to mean, I am special!'

I hadn't expected that, and I did ponder for a few moments as to whether I was going mad; perhaps I had developed a split personality disorder, but on balance, I decided I had probably not. Well, one of me did anyway.

Daisy was invisible to most people, could talk, cut his own toenails, and loved cheeseburgers; I just had to accept that and move on.

'I have an idea.'

'What?' said Daisy.

'I'll tell you all about it later.'

We walked back home in relative silence. I was thinking over what I should do next. Daisy was probably thinking about cheeseburgers. When we arrived back at Stanley Road, mum and dad were just getting ready to go out shopping in the car, so I said goodbye to Daisy and went off with mum, dad and Mags. It gave me time to think.

CHAPTER 14

Physio-Mechanics and The Plausible Deniability ploy.

Next day.

'Dad, I've accidentally kicked my ball over the garden wall into Mr Stanley's again. Can I pop round and retrieve it after breakfast?' I continued eating my cornflakes as if the request was of little consequence, but of course, it was.

Dad slowly lowered his newspaper and glanced at me suspiciously. He knew I was reasonably accurate when kicking my football.

Dad was becoming a little suspicious…

'How come you manage to consistently kick it over a ten-foot wall on that side of the garden but never over the six-foot fence on the other side?'

'I'm right-footed dad, so the ball is naturally inclined to bend to the left when I kick it, and of course, it's a brick wall - so when I boot it against the wall, it usually comes back.' I thought it was best to introduce some supporting details to burnish my explanation with some semblance of credibility....

'It doesn't come back when I kick it at the rickety old fence on the other side. It's all to do with physio-mechanics; I read that somewhere.' (I had no idea what it meant)

'Did you?' replied dad, questioning my use of the plausible deniability ploy. (I had no idea what that meant either) Apparently, when you have to tell an absolutely ridiculous lie, it's essential to include a tiny element of unquestionable truth carefully mixed in, making the lie almost believable. So I am told. If you smile nicely, you will always be given the benefit of the doubt.

It was all a load of old rubbish. Of course it was. The argument was seriously flawed, based solely on the assumption that I was always running in the same direction when I kicked the ball, which obviously I wasn't. I would have soon run out of garden - and he knew that. But there was just a hint of truth in my explanation, which made it sound sufficiently befuddling.

'I think you kicked it over the wall deliberately,' He countered, after a few moments of deliberation, completely disregarding my implausibly ludicrous excuse, which, in all honesty, was not an unreasonable conclusion.

I had expected some sort of challenge, so my backup excuse was already prepared... I always tried to have a backup excuse ready, just in case...

'No, dad, it was an accident. You know you want me to play for Chelsea, so I have to practice.'

It was a bit lame as far as explanations go, but it was the best I could come up with on the spur of the moment.

Dad mumbled something about being bamboozled with a load of old horse doodies and resumed reading his newspaper.

Mum scolded dad for using foul language, and a puff of white smoke gently rose up from behind his newspaper.

After breakfast, I popped round to Morti's.

I knocked on the door as usual, but today when Morti opened it, he was smiling, which was unnerving. It was the first time I had ever seen him do that.

'Hi Charlie, go on through. Daisy's outback somewhere.' I did.

I couldn't find him at first, so I made my way through the garden down towards the jetty.

'Charlie!' shouted Daisy from somewhere, but I couldn't see him.

'I'm up here.'

I glanced up and could just see him lying on a branch high up in an oak tree. He was much higher up than I had ever seen him climb before.

'What are you doing up there today?' I shouted.

'I'm looking for Nancy's canal boat. It must be easy to spot; it is painted bright pink.'

'It's somewhere in Oxford you idiot; that's about sixty miles away. You'll be lucky if you can see the horizon from up there, and that's only five miles away.'

'Well, I don't know, do I? and I don't know how far a mile is. It could be ten miles back to the house for all I know.'

'How far is a mile,' asked Daisy?

'It's not. Your garden is about a quarter of a mile from the house to the mooring, so it's two hundred and forty times longer than that.'

'What's two hundred and forty?' shouted Daisy.

I threw my hands up in the air and fell back on the grass in exasperation.

'I thought you were good at maths?'

'I am, but not that good. I'm still a lion, you know.'

There wasn't much I could say to that.

Daisy carefully climbed down the tree and eventually arrived a little worse for wear, having painfully encountered various branches on the way down.

'It's easy getting up… but I don't like the coming down bit. I forgot I didn't like heights.'

'I forgot I didn't like heights.'

I stared at Daisy in astonishment, totally dumbfounded by his act of stupidity.

'You don't like heights, but you climbed halfway up an oak tree?' You could have fallen and killed yourself.'

Daisy cowered with embarrassment at my reprimand. 'I forgot; it wasn't until I was up the tree and looked down that I remembered,' he meekly mumbled, peering up at me over the top of a paw.

'Well, you can't afford to forget. I will never be able to find Eleanor and Nancy without you.'

'If I can't see them from up there, how will we find them?' asked Daisy picking broken twigs and leaves out of his mane.

'In a way, which is less dangerous than climbing trees for a start,' I replied.

'How?'

'Well… I thought we could take the dinghy and row to oxford. That way, we could keep an eye out for pink canal boats on the way. They have got to stay on the river, haven't they?'

'I wouldn't have thought of that,' said Daisy, 'It's not very exciting or adventurous just looking. When my grandparents were in the jungle, they used to think up all sorts of devious ways to hunt for things, especially dinner.'

'Did they?' I asked.

'Oh yes. Sometimes they would hide behind a tree, then pounce on a baby antelope, and tear it to pieces for dinner.'

'That is horrible,' I exclaimed.

I could feel my eyes open wider and my mouth involuntarily fall open at the thought.

'Apparently, antelopes are quite tasty, a bit like chicken,' replied Daisy, 'but not as tasty as a cheeseburger. He licked his lips which unnerved me a bit. I had to shake my head in disbelief.

'What's that dreadful recollection got to do with finding Nancy?' I asked.

'Nothing really. I just thought I would mention it.'

'But why? I asked, sounding completely baffled.

'I don't know,' said Daisy. 'I just thought that…'

'Well, don't. It was ghastly.'

Daisy went into a huff for a few moments.

'Right,' I continued, 'what we will do is take the dinghy as I suggested and row up the Thames to Oxford.'

'You said that's a long way,' enquired Daisy.

'It is.'

'How long will it take?

'I don't' know about ten hours, I suppose.' I didn't really know how long it would take, but I had to make it sound achievable.

'I can't row for ten hours. I'll be totally knackered,' said Daisy. 'I don't mind rowing around the creek, but I wasn't expecting to row halfway round the world.'

I was about to explain how big the world was but then decided not to bother; it would have been too confusing for Daisy.

'I'll row half the way then,' I suggested.

'We've still got to row back. That's another ten hours.'

'Umm,' I mumbled. 'Alright, maybe rowing isn't the best idea… what if we ask Baggers and Fliss to give us a hand?'

'How?' said Daisy looking at me curiously.

'Well…' there was a long pause while I thought this through before opening my mouth. 'What if Baggers takes us in the dinghy on his back?'

'Brilliant,' said Daisy. 'So, no rowing at all. We can just sit back, take in the scenery and eat cheeseburgers; that would be wonderful.'

'And look out for the Pink Flamingo,' I added.

'Oh Yes, I forgot about that for a moment.'

'So, all we have to do now is convince Baggers to take us.'

'No problem,' replied Daisy. 'Why shouldn't he?'

'There might be something we haven't thought off.'

'Like what,' replied Daisy.

'Well, I don't know… I haven't thought of it yet, have I?'

'Why not?' asked Daisy, 'now's the time we need some blue-sky thinking.'

I didn't quite know how to answer that… so I didn't. It was another one of those *"answers on a postcard, please,"* moments.

'Right, let's go down and talk to Baggers and Fliss,' I suggested.

We wandered off down to the jetty to see if we could find Baggers, and luckily, when we got there, he was wafting about in the middle of the river.

'Baggers,' I shouted, but he couldn't hear me. 'He can't hear me, Daisy. What are we going to do?'

'I've got an idea,' said Daisy, wandering off into the trees. A few minutes later, he returned with a coconut.

'What the flup was that?'

'Watch!' instructed Daisy as he threw the coconut into the air. It landed two feet in front of Baggers's nose with a big splash. Baggers leapt out of the water, then fell back with another enormous splash sending a tidal wave in all directions.

'What the flup was that! ' shouted baggers.

'Hi Baggers,' I quickly interrupted. Sorry about that. We were just trying to attract your attention.'

'What, by knocking my bloody teeth out?' snapped Baggers, 'I'm having a quiet wallow in the mud, and you start throwing rocks at me.'

'It wasn't a rock; it was a small coconut, and I missed you by a mile,' shouted Daisy in his defence.

'Well, it felt like a rock,' replied Baggers, and that was not a mile. It nearly hit me. Anyway, what do you want?'

'Can you come in a little closer?' I asked, 'It's confidential.'

'You're not going to throw more coconuts, are you?' asked Baggers gingerly. He was, for obvious reasons, a little reluctant to come any nearer.

'No. I promise,' replied Baggers.

At that, Baggers started wafting through the water towards the riverbank.

'So,' said Baggers, now half out of the water and resting on the riverbank. He flashed Daisy a stern look of dismay, 'what is this confidential thing you want to talk about?' He sounded a little abrupt.

'We need your help to get to oxford,' I asked.

'Get a bus,' suggested Baggers.

'We can't do what we want to do on a bus,' I replied.

'What do you want me to do?' asked Baggers.

'Nothing much; we just want to sit in our boat, on your back and for you to swim slowly upstream to Oxford.'

Baggers looked to his left, then to his right, then in the sky before returning his gaze to me.

'You have been with that loony lion for too long. He has softened your brain.' He flashed an admonishing glance at Daisy, who was sitting very quietly, saying nothing.

'But it's important,' I said.

'Why?' replied Baggers.

'It's a complicated story,'

'Try me?' said Baggers.

So I told Baggers the whole story about Eleanor and Nancy's sudden disappearance and how Daisy and I had formed a private investigation agency.

'How long have you been a private investigator?' asked Baggers.

'Not long,' I replied a little coyly.

'Months?' asked Baggers.

'No, not months.'

'Weeks?'

'Not exactly.'

'Days then?' said Baggers.

'A few hours,' I replied meekly. I needed to end this painful interrogation.

'A few hours, Jumping Jehoshaphat's, ' exclaimed Baggers. 'I bet this is your first case, isn't it?'

'Sort of,' I replied. My replies to Baggers' questions were now almost in whispers.

'Sort of?' what does that mean?' he asked.

'Well, it's not exactly a case as such,' I replied.

'Not a case, then what is it?'

'Well, what it is, is I'm worried about Morti and why his wife and daughter suddenly disappeared, so I thought we would try to find them and ask them why they left.'

'Have you spoken to the police,' asked Baggers?

'Yes, they know all about it, but they can't do anything, and they won't tell Morti where they are because Eleanor and Nancy asked them not to.'

'Has Morti murdered them?' asked Baggers with a curiously squinty-eyed look in his eye.

'No. He has not. The police said they are alive and well, but they won't tell Morti where they are.'

'Well, in that case, what's the point?' they obviously don't want to be found.'

'I think they do,' I replied.

'Why?' said Baggers.

'Morti told me they were perfectly happy, and he doesn't understand why they left... He just wants to know why, which doesn't seem unreasonable, does it?'

'I suppose not,' replied Baggers mulling over my explanation. 'And if we do find them and they don't want to tell us anything, will that be it?'

'Absolutely,' I confirmed.

'What about the loony? I suppose he's coming?' Baggers still hadn't forgiven Daisy for the coconut incident.

'I might need him, and he is invisible, which is handy.'

'So am I, to the two-legged's,' replied Baggers.

'It could be a bit dangerous if we have to go walking about anywhere, you might knock a bus over.'

'That's nice,' said Baggers. I carry you all the way to Oxford, but I can't go for a wander around to look at the sites because I might knock something over.'

'You are quite cumbersome and a bit clumsy,' added Daisy.

'Not too cumbersome to dodge flying coconuts,' replied Baggers sharply.

'I've already apologised for that,' said Daisy.

Baggers didn't realise just how big he really was.

Baggers shook his head a couple of times, 'fair enough, I won't mention it again.'

'So, will you take us?' I asked.

'Yea, okay. When?' asked Baggers.

'Now's as good a time as any.'

'Right,' said Baggers, 'you two get in the boat and row to the middle, and I'll go and find Fliss. She hasn't had a day out for ages; she will probably enjoy this.' After a few minutes had passed, Baggers and Fliss returned.

'Hello, you two,' said Fliss, 'I hear we're going out on the river for the day?'

We're all off to the Sandbank...

'Yes, it should be fun,' I replied.

At that, Baggers gently lifted our boat a few inches out of the water and started the journey to the sandbank where the creek joined the River Thames. Baggers moved quite fast, faster than I expected. It felt odd ploughing along on top of the water without using the oars. Fliss waddled on behind without a care in the world.

'I could get to like this,' said Daisy, leaning over the side of the boat.

'We are on a case,' I replied 'it's not supposed to be a holiday.'

'Are we being paid?' asked Daisy.

'No, not exactly. It's a trial run to see how our partnership works out.'

'Oh, so it is a partnership then?'

'Yes, for now,' I replied.

'I'm so excited,' said Daisy. He did look very pleased with himself, 'I've never been on an adventure before.'

'It's not an adventure or a holiday,' I corrected, maybe slightly too sternly on reflection. 'We are just trying to find two people who, for some reason, decided to run away from their lives.'

'You don't have to be so serious about it,' said Daisy, 'I do know what this could mean to Morti. They were a happy family before all this happened. I saw it every day, and Nancy was very nice to me... never serious or stern like some people.' He lowered his voice for effect when he said the last few words and dropped his head slightly.

I glanced at Daisy and realised that my telling off was a little harsh, and perhaps I should try to lighten up a bit.

'I'm sorry Daisy, I'll be nicer in future.'

'Okay, partner,' replied Daisy with an enormous smile.

I must admit, he does make me smile, except when he's cutting his toenails. We were approaching the sandbank just before the junction with the main river when Baggers shouted to us...

'Hold on you two, I've just got to walk over the sandbank to get to the main river.'

At that, we rose out of the water as Baggers waddled over the sandbank. We steadied the boat by holding the oars against Baggers' back. Fliss happily waddled on behind, and then Noof arrived and settled on Fliss's back.

'Hey, what's happening, everybody?' asked Noof. 'Are we going on holiday?'

'I'm not sure,' replied Fliss, 'I think it's an adventure.'

Crossing the Sandbank to start their Journey.

'We are on a quest to find Eleanor and Nancy,' I shouted to Noof.

'Morti's wife and daughter?' asked Noof.

'Yes,' I replied.

'So what are we doing?' asked Noof.

'We are going to visit all the boat moorings on the river to see if anyone has seen Eleanor's canal boat,' I replied, 'it's bright pink, and it's called the Pink Flamingo.'

'Oh, right,' said Noof, 'do you want me to scout ahead?'

'Yes, that would be a great idea,' I replied.

'Better keep your voices down a bit,' said Daisy, 'Remember, we are all invisible except for you, so it might look a little strange if someone sees you shouting at nobody, they might think you have gone a bit do lally tat.'

Noof flew off upstream, but not before having a quick nibble on a snail on Fliss's back.

Slowly, Baggers and Fliss sank majestically back into the main river. From afar, all that could be seen was our boat skimming over the water with an eager desire to be somewhere else.

It must have mystified anybody who saw me as I wasn't rowing and didn't have an outboard engine. We cruised past a pleasure boat going in the same direction, and two people on the top deck gazed down, baffled by the speed at which I was travelling.

Charlie speeding across the water, baffling onlookers!

'I caught a current,' I shouted up to the bewildered day-trippers. But they didn't seem to believe that. I waved goodbye as they slowly faded away behind me.

'We should get to Kew Gardens in about half an hour,' said Daisy, 'there's a short term mooring facility there. We could ask around to see if anybody remembers seeing the Pink Flamingo?'

'How do you know that?' I asked. I was curious about how Daisy knew more than I did about canal boat mooring areas on the Thames.

'I checked on the internet,' replied Daisy, surprisingly unruffled by my question. He almost swept the question aside with his casual laissez-faire manner as if it were of no consequence.

'The internet?' I responded with astonishment, 'how do you type with those big paws? One paw must cover the whole keyboard.' I immediately realised I shouldn't have asked the question - I instinctively knew Daisy would come back with a smart answer.

'Oh, you are a silly, silly boy,' replied Daisy with the hint of an upper-class twang in his tone, 'it's all to do with having a decent education, old bean.'

'You never went to school,' I snapped back.

'Didn't say I did, but I have learnt how to use Siri on Morti's iPhone, and that's about as much education as anyone needs these days.'

'It knows everything; Siri is my best friend now.'

'But it only responds to the owner's voice,' I queried, believing I had found an obvious flaw in Daisy's explanation.

'No, she don't. You just have to speak in an authoritative but charming manner; it fools her every time, bit like most women.'

'Siri is my best friend,' said Daisy

Daisy displayed an unusually demeaning and slightly chauvinistic tone, an unattractive trait I hadn't noticed before, but then nobody was perfect.

I wondered if maybe he had had an unpleasant experience with a lady friend in the past. But then I realised that was highly unlikely in the circumstances as there didn't appear to be any other lions in Enigami.

'Are you sure about that,' I asked.

'Absolutely. Works every time.'

'Ahh,' I replied. I was flabbergasted and a little lost for words.

As dozy as I sometimes thought Daisy was, once again, he had produced a simple solution to what appeared to be an unsolvable problem but wasn't. Admittedly, throwing a coconut at Baggers to attract his attention wasn't one of his brighter ideas, but even that had worked.

'I just asked Siri where the canal boat mooring areas were from here to Oxford, and she printed them out for me.'

'But most other people can't hear you or see you?' I enquired gingerly.

'Siri can't see me, so she doesn't know who I am, and to be honest, she responds to just about anybody at a push. She's not that faithful to Morti, but that's flighty women for you.'

'What's a flighty woman?' I asked; having not heard the phrase before, I wasn't sure what he was alluding to.

'It's one that keeps flitting from one man to another,' replied Daisy, with a sombre moralising tone.

I suddenly twigged where this was going. 'Oh, you still think Eleanor has run off with another man?' The penny had dropped.

'Well, it is a distinct possibility,' replied Daisy.

'Did your girlfriend run off with somebody else?' I asked…

Daisy paused for a moment, 'you're too young for all that nonsense; I'll tell you all about girls another time.'

'Oh, right,' I mumbled, unsure whether I had been fobbed off about something I should know more about.

'If Eleanor has run off with another man, there isn't going to be much we can do about it, is there?' I asked. The seed of doubt had been planted.

'In all honesty, probably not,' replied Daisy, 'but we don't know that yet, do we?'

I was beginning to wonder if maybe I was sticking my nose into something I shouldn't. 'Do you think we should forget about all this and go back home?' I asked.

'Charlie, we've started this, so we might as well finish it. One way or another, we may find out why she left, then maybe, if it's good news, you can tell Morti what we found out.'

'And if it's not good news?' I added.

'Well, we've had a nice day out on the river….' Daisy smiled at me, 'and we say nothing. But we don't know anything yet… for certain.'

Daisy was right, so I sat back, looked at the scenery, and pondered over what might happen with Eleanor, Nancy, and Morti.

'There's Kew Garden's shouted Charlie.

After about fifteen minutes, Noof returned and sat on Fliss's back. 'Kew Gardens coming up, and there are lots of canal boats moored up.' 'Good,' I thought, we can actually start doing something positive. All the talk about Eleanor running off with another man had depressed me a little. The thought of it didn't seem fair.

As we came round the bend in the river at Richmond, I could see the top of one of the gigantic greenhouse's on the riverbank. I could also see several canal boats tied up on the bank.

'Right,' I said to Baggers, 'can you pull up here and shuffle around for a bit while I row to the shore and have a word with the boat owners.

Charlie and Daisy row to the riverbank.

'No problem,' replied Baggers. He slowed right down and slowly sank under the water.

Fliss then disappeared under the water, and Noof fluttered up into the air, surprised that his landing ground had suddenly vanished from sight.

The dinghy floated off, and Daisy started rowing towards the canal boat mooring area.

Noof flew over to Daisy and sat on his head. Daisy twitched but didn't say anything. Noof then started to ferret around on Daisy's head to see if there were any tasty titbits he could nibble on.

CHAPTER 15
Inconsequentiality and Friends.

I tied the dinghy up, and Daisy and I jumped out and started walking along the towpath to the canal boats.

'What should I do?' asked Noof, still sitting on Daisy's back.

'Could you look up ahead to see where we should go next?'

'No problem,' replied Noof. He flew off upriver towards Twickenham.

On the first boat we came to, an elderly couple were sitting on deckchairs drinking tea and eating sandwiches.

'Hello,' I shouted.

'Hello,' they replied.

'I wonder if you can help me?' I asked.

'Yes, of course, come on board.'

'We walked up the tiny gangplank to the boat and made our way to the aft deck where the couple were sitting.

'Would you like a cup of tea?' asked the lady. She was large, almost twice the size of her husband, and wore a bright red coat and a large red hat which, for some strange reason, I immediately thought would be very handy if she accidentally fell in the water. It would make her very easy to spot, a big red blob bobbing along in the river.

'That would be very nice,' I replied.

'I'm Irene, and this is my husband Ron,' said the lady. Ron smiled. He was tiny, about five foot six inches, exactly the same height as Irene, and dressed in a bright blue jacket, matching trousers, and a boater hat. I at once thought that they would make a super pair of giant garden gnomes. My dad collected gnomes, especially the ones with fishing rods.

Tea with Irene and Ron.

Our last garden was full of them because everybody gave them as Christmas or birthday presents. That's probably one of the reasons we moved. They were taking control of the garden, and we had to escape. That's what dad told us....

'I'm Charlie Christmas.'

'That's a nice name,' said Irene. So, Charlie Christmas, would you like a ham and cress sandwich with your tea?' she flashed me a motherly smile.

'Oh yes please,' I replied.

'Ask them if they have any cheeseburgers,' prompted Daisy. I don't like ham and cress; it's horrible. The cress tickles my nose.

'No.' I whispered, 'be quiet.'

'Sorry, said Irene, pinching her eyebrows, 'Did you say no? she sounded confused.

'My apologies,' I replied, 'My stomach was rumbling a bit. I was telling it to be quiet.' I smiled sweetly at Irene, then glared cretinously at Daisy. Irene glanced around to see who I was glaring at, but obviously, there was no one that she could see. She probably thought it was some sort of nervous tick or possibly that I was the village idiot having a day out.

'Yes please. I would love a ham and cress sandwich.'

Irene passed me a cup of tea and the sandwich and flashed me another motherly smile. Daisy turned his nose up at my sandwich, which I wasn't going to share with him anyway.

'Thank you,' I said, munching into the sandwich.

'So what are you doing rowing up the river?' asked Ron. 'Off to see some friends?'

'Yes, I am. I'm looking for a lady and her daughter, who live next door to me. They are cruising up to oxford on a canal boat called the Pink Flamingo. They came this way about nine months ago.'

'I don't suppose you remember seeing them.' I was being a little economical with the truth, but I thought it was necessary to avoid any awkward questions.

'Well, a pink canal boat would be very distinctive,' said Ron, 'hard to miss.'

'Did you see it?' I asked expectantly.

'No, definitely not,' replied Ron, who proceeded to eat his sandwich as if he hadn't eaten for days.

'Oh,' I replied, now a little deflated.

'But then we only came on holiday two weeks ago; your friends would have probably cruised by ages ago.'

'Um, yes,' I replied, 'you are probably right.

Do you know anybody who has been here for six months or longer?' I took a sip of my tea.

'There is a man on that boat up there,' said Ron. He pointed towards a green and yellow-painted boat with a Union Jack on the stern. It was much bigger than most of the other boats tied up along the bank.

'His name is Eric, but everybody calls him Mad Eric.'

'Is he dangerous?' I asked.

'No, just a bit strange by all accounts. But then you have to be a bit strange to live on the river.'

'Oh,' I replied. I made a note to remember that.

'We spoke to him about a week ago,' said Ron, 'he's been here for over a year from what I could make out.'

'I will have a word with him later,' I replied, 'thank you.'

'You seem very young to be out on your own,' queried Ron.

'I live next to the river a couple of miles back that way,' I pointed back to where we had just come from, 'you get used to being on the river every day when you live next to it.' I was fibbing a bit, but the last thing I needed was for Ron or Irene to mention any concerns they might have to the police about a boy on the river on his own. I wasn't, but they didn't know that.

I conveniently forgot to mention that I had only lived by the river for three weeks. Before that, I lived in Cheltenham, miles away from any rivers; in fact, I had never seen a river before coming to Chiswick.

'Of course you do,' acknowledged Irene. 'We come from Birmingham, there is a canal there, but we've never seen it.'

It went strangely quiet for a few minutes while we ate the sandwiches and drank the tea. It was a bit weird, just eating noises and slurping with the intermittent smiles of dining satisfaction.

'We are not as lucky as you living next to the Thames,' said Irene. I smiled and finished off my sandwich.

'So, you're a bit of a gumshoe, I presume?' asked Ron whimsically.

'Um?' I eventually replied once my mouth was empty, 'gumshoe, what's a gumshoe?'

'Gumshoe, it's an old fashioned name for a private investigator?' clarified Ron.

I glanced inquisitively at Daisy, but he just gave me a weird smile as if to say, "*don't look at me; I haven't said anything, and if I had, they wouldn't have heard it.*"

'Investigator?' I queried?

'You said you were looking for a lady and her daughter on what is a very long river, so you will have it all to do to find them.'

'Yes, I suppose I will, but I have got a couple of clues,' I thought I might as well play along with their misunderstanding of the situation. That was my first mistake

'Maybe we should employ you to search for our daughter,' said Ron. I noticed that he and Irene had suddenly taken on a more sombre appearance.

'Have you lost her?' I inquired, at once realising that that was another mistake. I should have just confirmed that I was simply looking for someone I knew and that I was not a private investigator, but I didn't, unfortunately. That is the dark hole you fall into when allowing inconsequential remarks to slip from your lips.

'Yes, we lost touch with Alison three years ago,' said Irene, 'she came down to London to work. She told us she was living on a houseboat on the River Thames.'

'At first, everything was fine, we had letters and phone calls, but then one day, it all stopped. We never heard from her again. Her mobile phone doesn't work anymore.'

'I am sorry,' was my immediate response, but those three words – probably the worst cliché in the world - always sound so inadequate and deficient for the intended purpose. They never really convey how you feel, perhaps because you don't really know how you feel at that particular moment.

'Thank you,' they chorused in grateful appreciation.

It was perfectly timed, poignant, and unnerving, almost as if they had rehearsed it for effect.

Ron, Irene and Alison.... The weeble family.

'So, you have no idea what happened to Alison?' I asked. For some bizarre reason, I imagined she would be a miniature version of her mum. A bit like a weeble, but a different colour, probably bright green. I began to conjure up visions of the three of them bouncing in the water, a red one and a blue one, followed by a smaller green one, all slowly disappearing from view.

Daisy looked at me in total amazement. He knew where this was heading, and it wasn't where we were supposed to be going.

'No, none at all,' they soulfully chorused again.

The depressingly woeful tone of their voices was heart-breaking. I went to a catholic mass once by mistake, and there was nobody else there except the priest and me. I am not a Catholic. The priest held up the chalice and kept looking at me, beckoning, beseeching, almost pleading with me to come up and take communion, but of course, I couldn't. The priest sounded just the same, lost and bewildered. It was as if he had been forsaken by his god – and that was how they sounded.

'Well, I can ask about her whenever we stop if that helps.'

'That would be wonderful,' muttered Irene.

'But London is a huge place. I'm not sure how much help that will be,' I confessed.

'It will be more than we've had so far from anybody else,' said Ron.

'Have you a photograph or any other information that I could take to help us with our investigation?' I asked.

'Us?' queried Irene innocently. Daisy looked at me in dismay.

'Sorry, I meant me; I'm on my own now, but sometimes I bring a friend along to help with the rowing, but he's not here today; he needs his rest as he is getting on a bit.'

I glanced at Daisy. He had fallen backwards and was laughing and waving his legs in the air with incredulous disbelief. I ignored him.

'You must be stark raving bonkers,' he muttered, 'we are not really private investigators; that was a joke!' He gazed at me in astonishment, 'and I am not getting on a bit either, thank you!' I think that annoyed him a bit. He was a bit gruff.

Daisy was not taking our investigation business very seriously.

Ron went down into the cabin and returned a few minutes later with a photograph and some copies of Alison's letters.

'Take these,' said Ron, passing me the documents, 'we have plenty of copies, and there's a note of our address and phone number if you need to contact us after we return home.

'I will do what I can,' I confirmed, 'I promise.' I could see they were becoming emotional talking about their daughter. Their expressions were the same as I had seen on Morti's face on the odd occasion when he didn't think I was watching him. A sense of helplessness and utter bewilderment morphing into the mental struggle of coming to terms with something for which there was no explanation.

'We must be leaving now; we have a lot of ground to cover today.'

'We?' queried Ron.

'Sorry, I meant me, me and my rowing boat, us, I'm very attached to my rowing boat...' it was a ludicrous explanation which probably only further enhanced the village idiot theory I mentioned earlier.

'Do take care and look after yourself,' said Irene.

'And your boat,' added Ron, with a quizzical expression.

'Thank you, I will,' I replied.

We walked back down the gangplank along the towpath towards the green and yellow-painted canal boat with the union jack.

'Emotionally attached to your rowing boat,' mumbled Daisy with a dubiously inquisitorial smirk.

'I couldn't think of anything else to say,' I replied, 'I keep forgetting they can't see you.'

'Emotionally attached to your rowing boat....'

'Probably for the best,' suggested Daisy, 'sometimes when you don't have anything to say, I find it's usually best to say nothing. They'd be joining you on the crazy farm if they saw you, a lion and two hippos having a cosy chat.'

I didn't think it was appropriate to refer to a mental asylum as a crazy farm anymore, but Daisy obviously didn't know that.

'And me,' added Noof, landing on Daisy's back.

'And you Noof, sorry, I forgot about you.'

'Everybody does,' replied Noof with a glum expression, 'except when they need me.'

'Cheer up, you old bugger,' said Daisy; 'we all need you.'

'Um,' said Noof.

'Did you see anything,' I asked.

'Yes, there are a few boats tied up there at the moment, but I couldn't see a pink one.'

'Never mind, we can ask around when we get there to see if anybody has seen it,' I replied.

'You do realise, we haven't got a snowball in hell's chance of finding any of them, don't you?' mumbled Daisy.

'I know,' I replied, 'but Morti is so sad, and so were Irene and Ron. I just thought we might just get lucky and find them.'

'You are getting too emotionally involved for this private investigation caper,' said Daisy.

'And what exactly does that mean?' I asked brusquely.

'It's becoming personal; *you got to remain outside the room to see what's going on inside.* Sam Spade said that in the Maltese Falcon; it's good, isn't it?' It's one of Morti's favourite films.

'What's the Maltese Falcon?' I asked. 'I had never heard of it.'

'It's a story about a private eye who takes on a case he shouldn't have, and his partner gets murdered.' Daisy glared at me with some obvious concern.

'Oh, I see,' I replied uneasily. 'Well, nobody is going to be murdered, least of all you. Somebody has to see you to murder you.'

Daisy went quiet for a moment while he digested that observation.

CHAPTER 16

Captain 'Mad as a Hatter' Eric

'Ahoy there shipmate!'

'Ahoy there shipmate,' I shouted as we arrived at the green and yellow-painted canal boat, but there was no reply.

'Ahoy there shipmate?' parroted Daisy with an expression of disbelief. 'Are we pirates now, as well as private investigators?' he mumbled in a mockingly sardonic tone that he could hardly contain.

'I was just using nautical terminology,' I replied. 'It's what sailors do when they're at sea.'

'We're not at sea, and we are not sailors,' replied Daisy. We are just floating up the river on the back of an invisible hippo - that hardly constitutes reasonable grounds for using a quasi-nautical greeting. You need to get a grip. Try using his name. He might think you're slightly deranged quoting trite seafaring expressions from Treasure Island.'

Eric suddenly appeared on deck smoking a pipe.

'Ahoy there, landlubber,' came a booming reply,' how can I help yee?'

'Yee?' said Daisy, 'What the flip is yee?'

'It's nautical language,' I replied with a smirk. Daisy threw up his paws in disbelief.

'Permission to come aboard, cap'n?' I replied.

Daisy winced.

'Permission granted me hearty,' rumbled Mad Eric's raucous voice. He was a large man, about twenty stone wearing a traditional French sailor's blue and cream horizontally striped jumper and, somewhat bizarrely, a pair of matching trousers, but the stripes were vertical. It was not a pretty sight. He wore a Captain's cap and was smoking a Gourd Calabash Sherlock homes type pipe. The traditional shaggy beard finished off the image of anybody who had ever lived on a boat but didn't have a clue how to sail it. The only thing missing was a black eyepatch, a cutlass and a wooden leg.

Daisy dropped his head and let out a sigh of despair. We walked along the towpath, up the gangplank and onto Eric's boat.

'So, what can I do for you, young man,' asked Eric in a booming tone.' I could feel his voice reverberate throughout the boat; it must have frightened the nearby fish. If there were any left that hadn't gone deaf.

'I was talking to some people further back down the towpath, and they said you may be able to help me find two people I am looking for.'

'Oh, and who might that be then?'

'Eleanor and Nancy Stanley. I think they passed this way about nine months ago.'

'Never heard of them!' replied Eric in his rumbling nautical manner. He sounded confident that he had never seen them. Then he took a long puff on his pipe.

'Oh,' I replied, obviously a little disappointed.

'Hmm,' muttered Eric, 'but many people pass this way.' He muttered the words in a deeply philosophical tone while slowly scratching his chin and gazing into the sky. It either meant something very moving and profound, or he was saying something blindingly obvious.

Then he adopted a contemplative posture with one hand resting jauntily on his waist like an old fashioned Toby jug and the other clasping his pipe.

'Their boat is painted bright pink; it's called The Pink Flamingo,' I added. Hoping that might spark some recollection.

'Ahh, now that is unusual,' replied Eric, 'You wouldn't forget that in a hurry.'

'You've seen them?' I exclaimed with measured jubilation, half expecting Eric to remember something after all.

'Nope!' Definitely Not. You don't see many pink canal boats - that's a bit different,' especially one called the Pink Flamingo, bit girly though.' He shook his head. 'To flamboyant for me.'

I didn't answer, but I did wonder why a pink boat was any more flamboyant than one painted bright green and yellow.

'No, hang on a minute, though….' Eric looked up to the sky again with a pained expression, obviously trying to recall something lost deep within the recesses of his memory.

Mad Eric tries to remember something, but it is hurting his brain.

Daisy looked upwards to see what Eric was looking at. I glanced at Daisy with open-mouthed astonishment.

'No, I did see a pink boat go past, and it would have been around February time. Come to think of it, there was a woman at the helm, attractive as I remember, but that's it. I don't know if that helps at all?'

'It does,' I replied, 'It helps a lot. Now we know she was definitely travelling in this direction.'

'You didn't speak to her at all, I suppose?' I asked.

'No. No, I don't think so, definitely not... no, hang on a minute, though.' He looked up to the sky again as if looking for divine inspiration.

Unbelievably, Daisy looked up again, 'what is he looking at?' asked Daisy nosily.

'Nothing,' I whispered.

'Nothing,' repeated Daisy, looking baffled.

'No,' continued Eric, 'I did speak to her for a few minutes, her and her daughter, I think.'

'What did they say?' I asked; I had a feeling this could be important.

'Wanted to know where she could buy some sausages.'

'Sausages,' I repeated, obviously sounding a little puzzled.

'Yes, said Eric, scabby old scragg ends of minced meat stuffed into a tube of intestines skin, you know the sort of thing.... delicious.'

I looked at him in utter disbelief that he had considered it necessary to explain, in detail, how a sausage was made. 'And that was it,' I asked, slightly deflated yet again and a bit sick.

'I told them about a butcher's shop I use further up the river.'

'Oh.'

'Nothing else?' I queried.

'No.'

I waited for a few moments just in case he had another banal revelation, but he didn't.

'Well, thank you very much for your help,' I said.

'Always happy to help a fellow seafarer,' replied Eric.

We left Eric humming the old sea shanty, *"what shall we do with the drunken sailor,"* and made our way back to the rowing boat.

'Well, that was a waste of time,' I mumbled under my breath.

'He was as mad as a box of frogs,' said Daisy, 'but at least we know where we can get some sausages; they might even have cheeseburgers?'

'Umm,' I replied.

We got back to the boat, and I rowed to the centre of the river and shouted out.

'Baggers, Baggers, where are you?'

Baggers's head popped out of the river.'

'Hello Charlie, how did it go?

'Rubbish,' I replied, 'but I know where we can get some sausages.'

'Sausages?' questioned Baggers sounding baffled.

'Forget it; it's not important.'

'Right,' said Baggers, still sounding a bit mystified.

'Can you take us a little further up the river?'

'No problem,' said Baggers. He turned and called out to Fliss.

'We're going further up the river love, come on.'

'Where's Noof?' I asked

'I think he is still in Twickenham,' replied Baggers.

'Oh well, we will probably run into him later,' I replied, 'let's go, Baggers,' so off we went to Twickers.

CHAPTER 17

Mona and The Maid of Killarney.

As we came round the bend at Twickenham, I could see Eel Pie Island. There were quite a few narrowboats moored up, so it looked like an excellent place to stop and ask about the Pink Flamingo.

'Can you drop us off here?' I asked Baggers.

'No problem,' he replied, slowly sinking away, allowing us to float off as before, and row the last forty yards to the shore.

I could see the top of Baggers and Fliss's head's as they cruised off to the middle of the river. Noof had returned and stood on Fliss's head on one leg while scratching his back with the other one. It was a peculiar sight to see. Noof appeared to be standing on the water.

I pulled the boat up on the shore, and Daisy and I jumped out and made for the towpath alongside where the narrowboats were moored.

The first boat we came to was The Maid of Killarney. She appeared to be a long way from home.

'What are we doing this time?' asked Daisy.

'Doing?' I questioned.

'Are we pirates or investigators?' asked Daisy.

'Oh, I see. Well, neither, as you've asked. I thought I would talk to them like normal people.'

'Well, that will be a novelty,' replied Daisy with a wry smile.

I made my way to the gangway of The Maid of Killarney and shouted out, 'Hello, is there anybody there?'

A lady popped her head up from the cabin, replying in a very strong Irish accent, 'Hello there, how can I help you young man?' She appeared to be relatively normal, definitely not like Mad Eric.

But maybe that was a little rude, I immediately thought afterwards. Eric may have been a bit scatter-brained and a little eccentric, but he did remember seeing Eleanor, eventually, and he had confirmed which way they were travelling and how sausages were made…

Mona.

But it was too late, I had had the thought, and I couldn't unthink it now. That was the problem with thinking too much. Sometimes I think about things I shouldn't think about, and then I am stuck with them whizzing about in my head, taking up valuable room, and I can't get rid of them. I remembered what Daisy had said a few weeks ago.

Don't get too clever too soon – Once you are clever, you must leave Enigami forever and never return.

The lady on the boat had enormous brown eyes and tiny little hands. On her head, she was wearing a green knitted hat with a large blue pompom over her bright red hair, which I didn't think went too well together. Her dress appeared to be knitted using half a dozen different colours, probably the bits and pieces leftover from other things she had knitted. It looked ghastly. Garish colours seemed to be a recurring sartorial theme for canal boat owners.

'I am looking for someone and wondered if you could help.'

'I don't know. You had better come on board and tell me more.'

We wandered down the gangway, and the lady beckoned me to come into the cabin.

'Take a seat, and you can tell me all about this person you are looking for, but before that, would you like a cup of tea?'

'Yes please,' I replied.

'My name is Mona, by the way; what's yours?'

'Charlie,' I replied.

'Charlie, yes, that will do; it suits you.' She smiled.

'I'm glad; it's the only one I have,' I replied cheekily.

Mona smiled back, 'Oh, I can see you could be a bit of a handful, me lad.'

'I think I'm a good person, though.'

Mona smiled again and looked at me for a few moments, 'Yes, I think you probably are.'

Tea with Mona.

I sat down on the bench, and Daisy laid down beside me. There wasn't quite enough room for both of us, so I pushed Daisy's bum a bit so I could sit down more comfortably. Daisy shook his head in frustration and pushed me further into the corner.

'Have you got enough room there? You appear to be squashed in the corner?' asked Mona.

'No, I'm fine,' I replied. I pushed Daisy's bum again, and she moved a couple of inches away.

Mona watched me with curiosity. She could obviously see I was a little person struggling to fit into a large space, and that didn't seem to make any sense, but then she didn't know about Daisy. I think she was beginning to have some concerns about inviting me on board.

Daisy wriggled a bit and moved back towards me, pushing me back into the corner again.

'Can I sit on that side,' I asked, 'I can't seem to get comfortable on this side?' I scowled at Daisy, and Daisy flashed me a triumphant grin.

'Of course you can,' replied Mona, 'I will make the tea.' At that, she wandered off to the galley halfway down the boat. I changed sides, still scowling at Daisy.

'You could sit outside,' I suggested. 'You're not much use in here,'

'That's charming; we wouldn't be here if I didn't row the boat.'

'You hardly did any rowing,' I swiftly replied, 'We sat on Baggers most of the time.'

'Umm,' shrugged Daisy, reluctantly agreeing.

I looked around the cabin and noticed that every flat surface, corner, nook and cranny was filled with delicate porcelain figurines and gleaming copper pots. I assumed that Mona must spend her days polishing the pots to keep them shiny and dusting the China figures. I began to imagine what would happen to them if the weather suddenly turned really windy and the boat began to rock. I could see thousands of pieces of broken China covering the floor and Mona on her knees, desperately trying to sort them out and glue them back together but getting it wrong. Figures with too many arms and not enough heads sprang to mind.

Fortunately, Mona returned with the tea tray and sat down, interrupting my meandering and increasingly bizarre thoughts.

'Milk and sugar?' she asked with a smile.

'Yes please,' I replied, 'you do have a lovely collection of China….' I commented. It was all I could think of to say.

'I do love the Capodimonte figurines,' Mona replied wistfully, 'they remind me of different times and better days when the world was a nicer place. When I look at them, I can almost imagine being where they are, somewhere that's more genteel and peaceful and where the world is a little less terrifying.'

'Isn't it now?' I queried. But I think that was maybe a bit naïve of me.

'No, not really, but then I don't know what it was like back in those days. Maybe it's just an illusion in porcelain….' Mona spoke wistfully. It was as if inhabiting the same space as the figurines had transported her to a different time.

'What would happen if the boat started to rock in the wind?' The words just fell out of my mouth. I didn't really want to ask that question; it just came out unexpectedly.

'Oh,' she replied with a disarming smile, 'That's not a problem.' She leaned over and pushed one of the figures, but it wouldn't move. 'I've stuck them all down with superglue. You could turn the boat upside down, and they'd still be in the same place.'

'That's a great idea,' I replied. I probably looked astonished.

'So, tell me about this person you are looking for?' Mona poured out a cup of tea and put a little milk in.' I'll let you put the sugar in.'

'Thank you.' Well, it's two people, actually. Eleanor Stanley and her daughter Nancy travelling to Oxford on a pink canal boat called the Pink Flamingo.'

Mona's eyes widened as soon as I mentioned the boat; something had piqued her interest.

'The Pink Flamingo,' said Mona curiously, 'Eleanor and Nancy Stanley.'

'Yes,' I confirmed.

'Eleanor and Nancy,' she repeated with a deeply inquisitorial gaze. So intense was the look in her eyes; I thought she was talking to someone sitting behind me.

'And why are you looking for these two people?' she asked, still casually sipping her tea. But something in her demeanour had changed, only very slightly, but enough for me to notice.

'I, that's my family and I, have just moved in next door to where the Stanley's live. And I got to know Morti, that's Mr Stanley. He told me that his wife and daughter suddenly left home nine months ago, and he hasn't heard a word from them since. He went to the police, and they managed to find Eleanor, but she told them she didn't want to go back home.'

'And that's it,' asked Mona.

'Yes, it all sounded very extraordinary. Morti doesn't know what made her leave, and I thought....'

'We!' interrupted Daisy, 'we are in this investigation agency partnership together, in case you forgot.' I gazed at Daisy for a moment but said nothing.

'Sorry, I meant we, that's my friend Daisy and me. If we spoke to Eleanor and Nancy, we thought we could find out why they left and maybe figure out how to get them to come back home. Morti has been so very sad.'

'Has he?' said Mona with a curious expression.

'Yes.'

Mona took another sip of her tea and stared at me for a few moments. I thought for a moment that maybe I had said something wrong.

'Have I said something?' I asked.

'No, no, you haven't, and Mortimer hasn't done anything either, and yes, I have seen them.'

'Have you?' I asked

'Yes, and there are things you don't know, which maybe you shouldn't, but as you are here with good intentions, perhaps you should. They may help you to understand what has happened.'

'When were they here?'

'About four months ago, they were moored up just next door for three weeks. We got to know each other quite well in a relatively short time. We spoke of many things.'

'What did they say?'

Mona was oddly reluctant to expand further, but paradoxically I could also sense her desperate need to tell me something. Her loyalty to Eleanor and Nancy and the absolute trust they had obviously placed in her were at odds with her divulging anything to me. Yet somehow, I knew she was about to tell me something important.

'Did Mortimer ever tell you about Eleanor's past?' asked Mona.

'What about her past?'

'Eleanor's mother and Eleanor's twin sister were both committed to mental institutions… psychiatric hospitals.'

'What exactly does that mean,' I asked. I was a little perplexed by the terminology. Daisy threw me a puzzled expression.

'Just that, they were both sectioned under the mental health act… and never released. They were considered too dangerous to be allowed back into the outside world as they might cause harm to other people.'

'Oh, I see, but how does that affect Eleanor and Nancy?'

'Eleanor thought that Nancy was going the same way when she started seeing things…. so rather than let her be locked up for the rest of her life like her mother and sister had been, Eleanor decided to take Nancy away and protect her from the world.'

'On the canal boat?'

'Exactly.'

'But surely Eleanor could have taken Nancy to see a doctor?'

'Yes, she could, but knowing only too well what had happened in the past, she knew there had to be a chance it might happen again, and it would be too late to turn back. She didn't want to lose Nancy, no matter what the cost.'

'But she can't know that for certain?'

'No, she can't, but she wasn't prepared to take that chance.'

'So what exactly was happening?' I asked, trying to make sense of it all.

'I don't know; she never told me the details. All she said was Nancy started to have schizophrenic delusions. She saw things that weren't there and began talking to people who weren't there.'

'Oh, I see,' this started me thinking.

'So I don't know if you finding her will be much help. Eleanor was devastated. She believes she may have passed down an incurable genetic madness to Nancy, and that's why they ran away.'

'But she hasn't; she has got it all wrong.'

Mona gazed at me confusingly. 'I'm not sure I understand?'

'I can't explain… you won't believe me if I told you… you would think that I was mad as well. Bum! I shouldn't have used that word.'

'I don't think Nancy is mad!' exclaimed Mona with a defensive glare that could have burnt holes through me.

'That's not what I meant to say; I'm sorry,' I replied, apologising profusely.

'Well, it sounded like it,'

'I can explain it to Eleanor and Nancy, but not to anybody else.'

'But why not me? I may be able to help.'

'You won't be able to; believe me.'

Mona was utterly baffled by my answer, but I could see she believed what I was saying, even though it didn't make any sense. She also seemed to realise that she may never completely understand what had happened.

'I should go now,' I said, 'I have to get back home for my tea.'

'But what about them?' asked Mona.

'We will start our search again tomorrow. What you have told me is important; I now know why they left.'

We left Mona feeling puzzled - and walked back to the rowing boat.

'So why do you think they left,' asked Daisy

'I have a good idea; I will let you know when I know for sure.'

'Okay,' said Daisy. 'Are you rowing or me?'

'Can you row?' I replied, 'my head hurts with all this thinking?'

I could see that Daisy wasn't too convinced by that excuse, but nevertheless, he rowed to the middle where we picked up with Baggers and Fliss, and they carried us back home.

CHAPTER 18

The greater our knowledge increases, the greater our ignorance unfolds.*

I was up bright and early on Sunday morning, ready for our trip to Oxford. I knew we (that's all the staff at the Charlie Christmas private investigation service) had a long day ahead of us, and there was a good chance that today, we might find Eleanor and Nancy.

'Going next door again?' asked Mags.

'Mags, I need to tell you something about Daisy....'

'Yes,' I mumbled. I knew what was coming next.

'You will have to take Mags round to meet Daisy sometime,' suggested dad.

'Yes, I will,' I had my fingers crossed.

'I could come round there with you today,' suggested Mags. She smiled nicely…

'No, not today - but some other time would be good.'

'I would love to come today,' pleaded Mags, noticeably disheartened by my rebuttal. 'I haven't met any new friends yet,'. Her enormous blue eyes mournfully implored me to change my mind. She knew that eventually, I always gave in to her pleading and once again, I succumbed.

'Oh, come on then,' I replied reluctantly, 'grab your coat, but I have to tell you about a couple of things first.'

'Okay,' she replied, saying nothing more. Mags smiled at me disarmingly. I loved her… how could I not give in.

'You two be back for dinner at four,' shouted mum.

'No problem,' I replied, but I wasn't sure if it was. We were probably going to cruise all the way to Oxford today, but I didn't have any idea how long that might take.

I knocked on Morti's door, and after a minute or so, Morti answered it.

'Hello, you two, and who might you be?' asked Morti, looking at Mags with a curiously sombre expression.

'Hello, Mr Morti,' said Mags quietly, 'I'm Mags,' she looked very nervous and slowly edged her way behind me.

I could see Morti's eyes getting smaller and his head growing larger; I thought it was going to explode.

Then he smiled. I was gobsmacked. 'Hello Mags,' said Morti, in a kindly tone, his beaming smile now spreading all over his face - his eyes grew larger, and his head started to shrink back down to normal size (or so it appeared).

I had never seen him this happy before. Something about Mags had brought out another side to Morti, one I didn't know he had. I also noticed that he said nothing about Mag's calling him Morti, but I still wasn't going to take a chance. Calling him Mortimer was just fine for me.

'So you are Charlie's little sister?'

'Yes, I am,' replied Mags.

'Charlie has told me all about you.'

'Oh, has he?' replied Mags glancing at me.

'It was all good,' he smiled again.

Mags smiled.

'Well, I hope you have fun playing with Daisy; she is perfectly harmless, and there is absolutely nothing to worry about, but no doubt Charlie has already told you that.'

Mag's looked surprised by Morti's unusual qualification, glancing curiously at me for a moment.

'I told you there were a few things you needed to know.'

'Um,' mumbled Mags gingerly.

We walked through the house and stepped out into the garden, but I stopped and turned to Mags before going any further.

'Look Mags, there is something I must explain now before we go any further.'

'Yes,' answered Mags with an innocence that worried me a little.

'Daisy is quite a bit bigger than most cats.'

'Is she fluffy?' asked Mags, which I found a little odd.

'Fluffy?' I repeated, 'Yes, he is quite fluffy, and she's a he, not a she.'

'But you call her…'

'I know what I call him, but that's the name that Morti gave him, and he seems quite happy about it, so….'

'No problem,' replied Mags demonstrating a hereto unforeseen blasé air of invincible inconsequence, 'let's go and find him?' she smiled.

'There is something else,' I continued warily.

'Oh,' replied Daisy. She still looked very fragile and vulnerable, and I really didn't know how she was going to react to my next revelation.

'Daisy's a…'

But before I could get the word out… the moment was snatched away.

Mag's meet's Daisy for the first time.

'Hi, Charlie, who's your friend?' asked Daisy, bounding towards us before screeching to a halt.

'Ah!' exclaimed Mags, flinching in amazement. 'You are a big cat,' she paused to catch her breath, 'and you are very fluffy.' Oddly, Mags didn't appear to be overly alarmed. I did wonder if her glasses were working properly.

'Daisy's a lion, not a cat, Mags,' I explained as best I could.

'Oh, I can see that… I'm not stupid, Charlie,' replied Mags with a condescending frown.

Daisy gazed intently at Mags and then at me, evidently looking for something, 'Did you bring the…?

'Yes,' I interrupted, 'I have your cheeseburgers.' I waved the bag. They were two that were left over from last night's dinner, which I had managed to smuggle out at breakfast time.

'I wondered where they went,' said Mags.

'And you can talk,' added Mags, looking at Daisy and then sideways at me with a curious expression. 'You never mentioned that.'

'That's just for starters,' I muttered.

'Well, that's nice. 'It will be lovely to have a new friend… someone I can talk to, even if you are a boy.'

Daisy didn't know how to take that.

'Right, we had better be going,' I said. 'I will explain what we are doing on the way to the boat mooring.'

'So what are we doing?' asked Mags after a few seconds.

'We have been searching for Mortimer's wife and daughter. They left over nine months ago without any explanation, but we think we know where they are, and we are going there today to find them and ask them why they left.'

'Oh, well, that sounds exciting,' said Mags.

'It might be a little dangerous, but some friends are coming along to help us.'

'That should be fun,' said Mags.

'Hmm,' I replied gingerly.

When we arrived at the jetty, Daisy jumped into the boat, sat down at the pointy end, and grabbed the two oars. Mags and I climbed in and sat down at the other end.

'So are you going to row all the way?' asked Mags.

'In a manner of speaking,' replied Daisy.

'You must be very powerful,' said Mags sounding impressed.

Daisy nodded his head nonchalantly, acknowledging the macho compliment.

'He's not that strong,' I muttered with a shrug.

Daisy rowed out into the middle of the stream, and I shouted out...

'Baggers!'

I couldn't see any movement anywhere, so I shouted again.

'Bagg..'

'Who is Baggers?' asked Mags.

At that, the boat began to rise slowly, and then Fliss popped her head up a few feet away.

'Morning everybody, are we all ready for the day trip?' asked Fliss.

'Morning, Fliss,' said Daisy.

'What's happening?' asked Mags, beginning to panic.

'It's alright; we are sitting on Bagger's back, he's a hippo, and he will take us up the river to Oxford.

'What?' exclaimed Mags, now, for the first time, sounding confused.

Mag's meets Bagger's, and Fliss

'I was going to mention Baggers and Fliss, they are hippos, and they talk, as well. They will carry us upriver, so we don't have to row all the way.' I glanced disparagingly at Daisy for telling the porky pie earlier.

'This is all becoming very weird,' said Mags, 'How come they all talk?'

'It's a long story. I will explain everything later; it's complicated.'

'Off we go then,' said Fliss dropping down so that just her eyes could be seen above the water, and off we went. Fliss upfront and Baggers behind with us sitting on top. Daisy was relaxing at the pointy end and had put his sunglasses on again.

We passed over the sandbank at the mouth of the junction with the main river and dropped back down into the Thames to continue our journey up the river.

'This is fun,' said Mags, obviously enjoying herself. 'Better than sitting at home playing with my dolls.'

'Headless dolls,' I added in a muted tone, 'and anyway, aren't they just bodies, dead bodies at that, if they don't have heads?' It was a blunt comment, but I thought I should make my views known about Mags's curious beheading ritual performed on defenceless dollies. I still found it extremely uncomfortable.

'They don't need heads to wear dresses,' snapped Mags, as if we had somehow drifted into a fashion phase where heads were no longer an imperative.

'But I thought the whole point was....' I didn't go any further; this was an argument I would never win. But it still concerned me.

'The heads still glare at me,' muttered Mags as an afterthought.

'Do they?'

'Yes.'

'Well, I suppose they are a little put out by....' I didn't finish... 'Anyway, what do you do with them?'

'I keep them in a drawer in my bedroom.'

'Oh, I see,' but I didn't.

'Are Baggers and Fliss married?' asked Mags.

'I don't know, I suppose so. Sometimes they do things in the water, and I think you have to be married to do that.'

'What do they do?' asked Mags.

'Things that grown-ups do,' I replied.

'But they're hippos that can't be the same.'

'Try telling them that,' I replied, possibly sounding slightly irritated by the constant questioning.

'I don't ask them silly questions; I just take it for what it is.'

'What a peculiar situation?' said Mags.

'Not really; this is Enigami. It's just a different world to the one we normally live in, but we are only passing through it for a short while.'

'So this won't last?' asked Mags.

'No. None of this lasts forever.'

Oh,' said Mags. I could see her brain formulating her next question…

Cruising up the river at a rate utterly inconsistent with the average speed of a rowing boat, we must have appeared a curious sight. Deep down, I felt we might be lucky today, and we would find Eleanor and Nancy. We passed by Ron and Irene's boat near Kew Gardens. They were both sitting on the deck having breakfast.

Waving at Ron and Irene and we pass by.

'Hello Charlie,' shouted Ron, 'is this the big day?'

'Yes, hopefully, we're going all the way to Oxford today.'

'Good luck; I hope you find them, don't forget to keep an eye out for our Alison.'

'I will,' I shouted back, although I didn't hold out much hope there. We didn't even know if she was on the river.

'I see you have your assistant with you today,' said Irene.

'No, that's just my sister; she makes the tea.'

Mags glared at me.

'Hopefully, we will see you tonight when you come back,' said Ron, 'pop in for a cup of tea if you have time.'

'We'll try,' I replied.

'Mad' Eric was singing a sea shanty as we passed.

We carried on a little further, and then we saw Mad Eric's Green and Yellow painted boat. Eric was standing on the deck playing the concertina and singing something, but I couldn't make out what.

Eric spotted us and stopped playing for a moment.

'Ahoy there landlubbers,' he shouted, 'off to Oxford?'

'Yes, we are.'

'Well, good luck, and watch out for pirates; they will nick anything.'

I wondered what a pirate would do with a rowing boat; it wasn't quite the image I had in my head.

Eric started playing the concertina again and continued singing another odd sea shanty, something to do with mermaids. I waved goodbye as he slowly faded into the distance.

'We'll be passing Mona on The Maid of Killarney at Twickenham next,' I said. 'Keep an eye out for her washing line.'

'Why?' asked Mags.

'She knits everything she wears in bright colours; you can't miss her.'

'You have met some very curious people,' said Mags.

'Don't forget the sausage shop,' interrupted Daisy, 'I wouldn't mind another cheeseburger.'

'We are not stopping for burgers. We've only been going for an hour; there's still a long way to go.'

'Oh,' said Daisy looking utterly disappointed by that announcement.

I turned to Mags, 'You are right; we have met some curious people, but they are all nice people, and they are all trying to help us.'

Mags didn't reply but just mulled over what I had said. As we entered Twickenham, I could see The Maid of Killarney on the right bank, so I shouted to Baggers....

'Baggers, can you slow down a bit as we pass the next canal boat?' It felt odd shouting at the water, but it usually worked.

I wasn't sure if Baggers had heard me, but then Fliss popped her head up.

'Hi Charlie, Baggers has just told me he is slowing down.'

'Thank you,' I replied. I wondered how Baggers and Fliss communicated under the water. As far as I was aware, they weren't using mobile phones, but anything was possible in Enigami.

As we slowly passed "The Maid", I could see Mona hanging up some washing. Everything, including her socks, bras, knickers and an assortment of woolly hats and jumpers, were bright green, red or orange.

Vomit and carrots!

185

'Ahh,' said Mags, 'That's ghastly; it looks like a washing line of vomit and carrots.'

Luckily, I don't think Mona heard Mags.

'Hi Mona,' I shouted.

'Hi Charlie,' she replied, 'off to find Eleanor and Nancy?'

'Hopefully,' I replied.

'I see you have a friend with you today.'

'My sister Mags,' I replied.

'Hello Mags,' said Mona.

'Hello Mona,' said Mags. I love your washing; very colourful.'

'Thank you Mags.

'Well, good luck, let me know how you get on,' said Mona.

'Will do,' I replied.

Molesey Lock and Baggers was getting a bit frisky

We cruised on, but the vision of the washing line remained in my head for some time, along with Mags's comment.

After Twickenham, we came to the first lock gate at Molesey.

I thought this might be a problem, but the lockkeeper saw us and opened the lock and in we all went. When we came out the other side, I shouted out to Fliss, and she surfaced.

'You called,' said Fliss

'Yes, I just wanted to make sure you and Baggers were okay going through the lock.'

'No problem,' said Fliss. It was getting a bit intimate in there at one point, all touchy-feely, but I put Baggers in his place, so no more funny business.'

'Right,' I replied a little warily. Not a hundred per cent sure what the "funny business" was.

'How many more locks till we get to Oxford?' asked Fliss

'I think it's around about twenty; why?'

'I don't know if I can hold him off that long.'

'Oh, I see…. Well, we may get lucky; Eleanor may have moored up before Oxford.'

'Let's hope so,' replied Fliss.

CHAPTER 19

Homecoming

The Pink Flamingo.

We travelled on through seven more locks until we reached Romney lock just outside Windsor, and then I saw it. The Pink Flamingo moored up just the other side of the lock gate.

'There she is Daisy,' I excitedly exclaimed, pointing at the canal boat we had been searching for.

'Good, now we can find out what happened,' said Daisy.

'Baggers,' I shouted, and Baggers dropped away from under our boat and popped up on one side.'

'Hi Charlie, is it lunchtime?'

'No, but we have found the Pink Flamingo.'

'Excellent.'

'If you two would like to play around here for a while, Daisy, Mags and I will go and see if they are in.'

'Okay,' said Baggers. Fliss smiled.'

I rowed over to the towpath and tied up the dinghy.

'Come on then, let's go and speak to them.'

Daisy looked a little reluctant at first. 'Are you sure this is the right thing to do?'

'Of course it is. They could answer many unanswered questions.'

'But will anybody be any better off?' asked Daisy

'I don't know,' I replied.

'What are all these questions,' asked Mags.

'I did tell you this was complicated.'

'I know you did, but you didn't explain,' replied Mags.

'Well, in a nutshell, Eleanor and Nancy disappeared nine months ago..'

'From next door,' asked Mags

'Yes, Eleanor is Morti's wife, and Nancy is his daughter, and we are here to find out why they left and if we can get them to come home.'

'Oh, I see.'

'And hopefully, find a cheeseburger along the way,' mumbled Daisy.

'A what,' said Mags; she thought she heard that wrong.

'A cheeseburger,' Daisy loves them, even though he's a vegan.'

'But vegans don't eat…'

'That's another story; I'll tell you all about it on the way back home.'

'Right,' said Mags.

We walked along the towpath to the gangplank next to the Pink Flamingo and stood at the bottom.

'Here we go then,' I said, crossing my fingers.

'Hello! is there anybody there?' I shouted

189

There was no reply, so I called again.

'Hello! is there…'

'Hello, can I help you?' A lady, who I presumed was Eleanor, came up through the cabin hatchway. She appeared friendly and gave me a welcoming smile. I smiled back. Unlike most canal boat people, she was nicely dressed, not too many colours.

'Hello, my name is Charlie Christmas, and this is my sister Mags. Could we come on board and speak to you for a moment?' I asked.

'What about?' she replied, appearing a little guarded, 'you're not selling anything, are you? We get a lot of hawkers around here.'

'No. No, we're not selling anything; it's more personal than that. It's about something I need to explain.'

'Well, you had better come on and tell me all about it,' said Eleanor, becoming a little more curious. Mag's and I walked down the gangplank and jumped on board. Daisy trailed on behind and jumped up onto the top of the cabin.

I was reluctant to jump straight in and mention Morti. I thought it might alarm Eleanor. So I decided to approach the subject from a slightly different angle.

'I, that's my sister Mags and I….'

'Hello,' interrupted Mags with a beaming smile, which to a certain degree was probably reassuring, 'I'm Mags.'

'Hello Mags,' replied Eleanor cautiously.

'Well, Mags and I,' I continued, 'we have just moved into number three Stanley road, Chiswick.' I let that sink in before going any further.

'Oh, I see. Well, that's nice.' Eleanor smiled again but was still unsure where this was heading. She also didn't appear to recognise the address I had mentioned.

'Didn't you live next door at number one?' I asked gingerly.

'Me? No, you must have me muddled up with someone else.'

'Aren't you married to Morti... Mortimer Stanley?'

'Who are you?' Eleanor's tone changed as she brusquely replied.

'I'm Charlie Christmas, and this.../'

'I know what your names are; you just told me that. What I meant was, who are you, why are you here, pestering me?'

'We are friends of Mortimer Stanley, your husband.' For one fleeting moment, I wondered whether I had made a terrible mistake. Maybe Eleanor had sold the boat to this lady and had moved on. Perhaps this private investigation work wasn't as easy as I thought after all. The doubts began to pile up in my head.

'Look, I don't want to be rude, but this is nothing to do with me,' said Eleanor, 'I think you had better go. You have made a terrible mistake.'

I said nothing for a few seconds; I could see Eleanor was becoming more agitated.

'Can I just explain something to you about Nancy?'

'Nancy?'

'Yes, your daughter Nancy.'

'How do you know...'

At that, Nancy appeared from below deck. Which was a little reassuring for me, considering my previous concerns.

'Hello, I'm Nancy, did someone call me....' She stopped talking the moment she saw Daisy.

'He's there, mum, on the top of the cabin,' exclaimed Nancy. An expression of distress flashed across her face.

'Hi Nancy,' said Daisy calmly, 'long time no see.'

'He's talking to me mum; he is real,'

191

Mag's me and Daisy meet Eleanor and Nancy at last.

'Nancy, it's me, Daisy, your friend,' said Daisy.

'Can you leave,' repeated Eleanor, 'you are frightening Nancy?'

'The lion is real, Mrs Stanley,' I replied unequivocally, 'I can assure you he is here, Nancy is not hallucinating, but only certain people can see him.'

'What?' exclaimed Eleanor, now utterly confused by what was happening. 'What do you mean the lion is real? I can't see any lion; it's imaginary, not real, and how did you know about Nancy's hallucinations? This is all madness. This is why we ran away.'

'I can see the lion,' I reiterated, 'Mags can see the lion, and Nancy can see the lion, but you can't, you never will.'

'I am here, you know,' said Daisy sounding a little irked. 'I can speak for myself; I thought we'd established that much.' Daisy had obviously taken offence at the condescendingly insensitive way I had spoken about him.

'I don't understand what is happening,' said Eleanor as she sat down, 'Why are you talking to somebody who isn't here?'

'Daisy is here, Mrs Stanley, but you can never see him because….' I replied.

'Because, because of what,' interrupted Mrs Stanley sharply.

'Because you are too old, and the world in which Daisy and his friends live can only be entered into by children, innocent children. And even they have to leave that world once they are thirteen years old. None of us is hallucinating; it's all to do with something that happened many years ago in Africa, and part of what happened came back to Number One Stanley Road.'

'Why thirteen?' queried Eleanor, no longer appearing as distressed as she was earlier.

'Because we learn too much by then. The space in our brain necessary for our imagination to maintain this other world is gone, filled with other boring, less important things.'

'So, what exactly happened at Number One?' asked Eleanor, the pieces of the puzzle slowly falling into place.

'When did Nancy first mention Daisy?' I asked

'About a year ago, maybe a little longer.'

'When she was what, ten years old?'

'Yes,' Eleanor confirmed.

'And you thought she was hallucinating?

'Yes,'

'And you thought she was going mad like your mother and sister?'

'How did you know that?'

'We spoke to Mona on the Maid of Killarney.'

'She promised to keep my secret,' replied Eleanor sounding disappointed.

'We explained some of what had happened, and she began to understand. That's why she told us how to find you.'

'So is it right what she said? I asked.

'Yes, it is. I thought the madness must be hereditary.'

'But you are not affected?'

'No. no, I'm not.'

'But you thought Nancy was?'

'Yes, I did,' but I'm not so sure now.'

'And you ran away with Nancy because you didn't want her taken away from you.'

'That's right.'

'Has she ever seen Daisy or the hippos since you left Number One?'

'No, she hasn't mentioned them.'

'So can't you see, Nancy wasn't going mad, just the opposite. She suddenly found she had access to another world, Enigami, and like me, she liked going there.'

'I can see that now, but you can see how it looked to me?'

'Yes, I can. So can you now go back home to Morti?'

'Morti?' exclaimed Eleanor, with a slight glimmer of a grin, 'does he let you call him Morti?'

'Oh no, absolutely not. Mortimer is the best I can get away with.'

Eleanor smiled. 'He's a good man, I hated running away, but I couldn't lose Nancy, not like I lost my mother and my sister.'

'Well, that's not going to happen now, is it?'

'So, if I am not going mad, can we go home to dad?' asked Nancy, who had been chatting away to Daisy.

'Yes, we can go home, and you can play with Daisy all you like.'

'Is anybody going to buy me a cheeseburger,' asked Daisy.

'I will get you one,' said Nancy, 'in fact, I will get you two.'

'What about us?' blurted Baggers and Fliss resurfacing.

'You too. I will get everybody cheeseburgers.'

'They are there, mum,' exclaimed Nancy pointing at Baggers and Fliss,' they are my lovely, gorgeous hippo friends, and I love them.'

'I can feel their presence Nancy,' whispered Eleanor.

Fliss blushed, and Baggers went strangely coy for a moment, apparently unaccustomed to compliments.

'I believe you now,' said Eleanor. 'I can't see them, but I can sense their presence, and it is strong.' She smiled at Nancy.

'What about me?' asked Daisy.

'You as well; I love you all,' replied Nancy, 'So, are we going home, mum?'

'Yes, yes we are,' replied Eleanor. 'I will sort out a few things on the boat, then we will turn her around and go back home.'

I smiled.

Daisy smiled.

Baggers and Fliss smiled.

Noof suddenly swept down from nowhere and landed on Baggers.

'So are we off to Oxford?' said Noof.

'No,' I replied, 'We've solved the mystery, and now we are all going home.'

'Oh, good,' replied Noof, 'It's a bit hectic out there today; there are some weird birds flying around. Some with no wings. He paused for a few seconds... 'Can we pick up a cheeseburger on the way home?'

'Yes,' replied Nancy, I'll get you one as well.'

'Jolly good,' replied Noof, with a big smile. 'I do love cheeseburgers.'

'Do you want to come back with us?' said Eleanor.

'No, it's okay,' I replied, 'Baggers will give us a lift.'

'Oh,' said Eleanor, still not totally convinced.

Daisy, Mags and I walked back down the gangplank back to our dinghy, and we all jumped in. Baggers lifted us up, and off we went.

It had been a good day; in fact, it had been a brilliant day for us all, but I would be glad to get back home and have a rest until next weekend. And Eleanor and Nancy would be back with Mortimer, so our first case had been a success, and I felt good, very good. Enigami was a wonderful world, and I was looking forward to my next investigation.

The End
(but only of this story)

Acknowledgements to W.B. Yates, Bob Dylan, J.F. Kennedy and Stevie Smith.

Coming soon….

CHARLIE CHRISTMAS

AND THE

ALISON BAINBRIDGE
MYSTERY.

Chapter one

Daisy rowed out to the middle of the water and whistled for Baggers and Fliss. The boat slowly lifted out of the water.

'Where to?' asked Fliss.

'Oxford,' I replied.

'Why Oxford,' asked Baggers?

'Another adventure,' I replied.

'Oh,' replied Baggers, looking a little concerned.

'We are going to find Alison,'

'Oh,' said Baggers.

And so, we started our next journey.

But today would be a little different as Nancy and Mags were coming with us. They had joined the Charlie and Daisy Private Investigation business.

Printed in Great Britain
by Amazon

81146492R00119